Classics.

# Little Women

## Louisa M. Alcott

*Abbey Classics*

PRINTED IN ROMANIA

# CHAPTER ONE

## PLAYING PILGRIMS

"Christmas won't be Christmas without any presents," grumbled Jo, lying on the rug.

"It's so dreadful to be poor!" sighed Meg.

"I don't think it's fair for some girls to have pretty things, and other girls nothing at all," added little Amy, with an injured sniff.

"We've got father and mother, and each other anyhow," said Beth contentedly, from her corner.

The four young faces on which the firelight shone brightened at the cheerful words, but darkened again as Jo said sadly, — "We haven't got father, and shall not have him for a long time." She didn't say, "perhaps never," but each silently added it, thinking of father away where the fighting was.

Nobody spoke for a minute; then Meg said in an altered tone, — "You know the reason mother proposed not having any presents this Christmas was because it's going to be a hard winter for everyone; and she thinks we ought not to spend money for pleasure when our men are suffering so in the army. We can't do much, but we can make our little sacrifices," and Meg thought regretfully of all the pretty things she wanted.

"I don't think the little we should spend would do any good. We've each got a dollar, and the army wouldn't be much helped by our giving that. I agree not to expect anything from mother or you, but I do want to buy Undine and Sintrum for myself," said Jo, who was a bookworm.

"I planned to spend mine in new music," said Beth with a little sigh.

"I shall get a nice box of drawing pencils; I really need them," said Amy decidedly.

"Mother won't wish us to give up everything. Let each buy what we want, and have a little fun; we work hard to earn it," cried Jo.

"I know I do — teaching those dreadful children nearly all day, when I'm longing to enjoy myself at home," began Meg.

"You don't have half such a hard time as I do," said Jo. "How would you like to be shut up for hours with a nervous, fussy old lady, who keeps you trotting?"

"It's naughty to fret, but I do think washing dishes and keeping things tidy is the worst work in the world. My hands get so stiff, I can't practise good a bit." And Beth looked at her rough hands with a sigh.

"I don't believe any of you suffer as I do," cried Amy; "for you don't have to go to school with impertinent girls, who laugh at your dresses, and label your father if he isn't rich."

"If you mean *libel*, I'd say so, and not talk about *labels*, as if pa was a pickle-bottle," advised Jo.

"I know what I mean, and you needn't be 'statirical' about it. It's proper to use good words, and improve your *vocabulary*," returned Amy with dignity.

"Don't peck at one another, children. Don't you wish we had the money papa lost when we were little, Jo? Dear me, how happy and good we'd be if we had no worries," said Meg.

4

"You said the other day you thought we were a deal happier than the King children, for they were fighting and fretting all the time, in spite of their money."

"So I did, Beth. Well, I guess we are; for though we do have to work, we make fun for ourselves, and are a pretty jolly set, as Jo would say."

"Jo does use such slang words," observed Amy, with a reproving look at the long figure stretched on the rug. Jo sat up, put her hands in her apron pockets, and began to whistle.

"Don't, Jo; it's so boyish."

"That's why I do it."

"I detest rude, unlady-like girls."

"I hate affected, niminy-piminy chits."

"Birds in their little nests agree," sang Beth, the peace-maker.

"Really, girls, you are both to be blamed," said Meg. "You are old enough to leave off boyish tricks, and behave better, Josephine. Now you are so tall, and turn your hair up, you should remember that you are a young lady."

"I am not! And if turning up my hair makes me one, I'll wear it in two tails till I'm twenty," cried Jo, pulling off her net, and shaking down a chestnut mane. "I hate to think I've got to grow up and be Miss March and wear long gowns, and look as prim as a China-aster. I can't get over my disappointment in not being a boy, and it's worse than ever now, for I'm dying to go and fight with papa and I can only stay at home and knit like a poky old woman;" and Jo shook the blue army-sock till the needles rattled like castanets.

"As for you, Amy," continued Meg, "you are altogether too particular and prim. Your airs are funny now, but you'll grow up an affected little goose if you don't take care."

5

"If Jo is a tomboy, and Amy a goose, what am I, please?" asked Beth.

"You're a dear, and nothing else," answered Meg warmly; and no one contradicted her, for the "Mouse" was the pet of the family.

Margaret, the eldest of the four, was sixteen, and very pretty, being plump and fair, with large eyes, plenty of soft brown hair, a sweet mouth, and white hands, of which she was rather vain. Fifteen-year-old Jo was very tall, thin, and brown, and reminded one of a colt; for she never semed to know what to do with her long limbs. She had a decided mouth, a comical nose, and sharp grey eyes. Her long, thick hair was her one beauty; but it was usually bundled into a net, to be out of her way. Round shoulders had Jo, big hands and feet, a fly-away look to her clothes, and the uncomfortable appearance of a girl who was rapidly shooting up into a woman and didn't like it. Elizabeth or Beth, as everyone called her — was a rosy, smooth-haired, — bright-eyed girl of thirteen, with a shy manner, a timid voice, and a peaceful expression, which was seldom disturbed. She seemed to live in a happy world of her own, only venturing out to meet the few whom she trusted and loved. Amy, though the youngest, was a most important person — in her own opinion. A regular snow maiden, with blue eyes, and yellow hair curling on her shoulders; pale and slender, and always carrying herself like a young lady mindful of her manners.

The clock struck six; and Beth put a pair a slippers down to warm. Somehow the sight of the old shoes had a good effect upon the girls, for mother was coming. Meg stopped lecturing, and lit the lamp, Amy got out of the easy-chair without being asked, and Jo forgot how tired she was as she sat up to hold the slippers nearer to the blaze.

"They are quite worn out; Marmee must have a new pair."

"I thought I'd get her some with my dollar," said Beth.

"No, I shall!" cried Amy.

"I'm the oldest," began Meg, but Jo cut in with a decided, —

"I'm the man of the family now papa is away, and I shall provide the slippers."

"I'll tell you what we'll do," said Beth — "Let's each get her something for Christmas, and not get anything for ourselves."

"That's like you, dear! What will we get?" exclaimed Jo.

Everyone thought soberly for a minute; then Meg announced, "I shall give her a nice pair of gloves."

"Army shoes, best to be had," cried Jo.

"Some handkerchiefs, all hemmed," said Beth.

"I'll get a little bottle of Cologne; it won't cost much, so I'll have some left to buy something for me," added Amy.

"Let Marmee think we are getting things for ourselves, and then surprise her. We must go shopping tomorrow afternoon, Meg; there are lots to do about the play for Christmas night," said Jo.

"I don't mean to act any more after this time; I'm getting too old for such things," observed Meg.

"You won't stop, I know, as long as you can trail round in a white gown with your hair down, and wear gold-paper jewellery," said Jo. "We ought to rehearse tonight. Come here, Amy, and do the fainting scene, for you are as stiff as a poker."

"Glad to find you so merry, my girls," said a cheery voice at the door, and actors and audience turned to welcome a stout, motherly lady, with a "can-I-help-you" look about her.

"Well, dearies, how have you got on today? Has anyone called, Beth? How is your cold, Meg? Jo, you look tired to death. Come and kiss me, baby."

While making these maternal inquiries, Mrs. March got her wet things off, her hot slippers on, and sitting down in the easy chair, drew Amy to her lap. The girls flew about, trying to make things comfortable. Meg arranged the tea-table; Jo brought wood, dropping, overturning, and clattering everything she touched; Beth trotted to and fro between parlour and kitchen, quiet and busy; while Amy gave directions, as she sat with her hands folded.

As they gathered about the table, Mrs. March said with a happy face, "I've got a treat for you after supper."

A bright smile went round like a streak of sunshine. Beth clapped her hands, regardless of her hot biscuit she held, and Jo tossed up her napkin, crying, "A letter! Three cheers for father!"

"Yes, a nice long letter. He sends all sorts of loving wishes for Christmas, and an especial message to you girls," said Mrs. March.

"I think it was so splendid in father to go as a chaplain when he was too old to be drafted, and not strong enough for a soldier," said Meg.

"Don't I wish I could go as a drummer, or a nurse," exclaimed Jo, with a groan.

"When will he come home, Marmee?" asked Beth, with a little quiver in her voice.

"Not for many months, dear, unless he is sick."

They all drew to the fire, mother in the big chair with Beth at her feet, Meg and Amy perched on either arm of the chair, and Jo leaning on the back. It was a cheerful letter, full of lively descriptions of camp life, marches, and military news; and only at the end did the writer's heart overflow with fatherly love and longing for the little girls at home.

"Give them all my dear love and a kiss. Remind them that while we wait we may all work so that these hard days need not be wasted. I know they will be loving children to you, fight their bosom enemies bravely, and conquer themselves so beautifully, that when I come back to them I may be prouder than ever of my little women."

Everybody sniffed when they came to that part; Jo wasn't ashamed of the great tear that dropped off the end of her nose, and Amy never minded the rumpling of her curls as she hid her face on her mother's shoulder and sobbed out, "I am a selfish pig! but I'll truly try to be better."

"We all will!" cried Meg. "I think too much of my looks, and hate to work, but won't any more."

"I'll try and be what he loves to call me, 'a little woman,' and not be rough and wild; but do my duty here, instead of wanting to be somewhere else," said Jo, thinking that keeping her temper at home was a much harder task than facing a rebel or two.

Beth said nothing, but wiped her tears with the blue army sock, and began to knit with all her might, losing no time in doing the duty that lay nearest her.

Mrs. March broke the silence that followed Jo's words by saying in her cheery voice, "Do you remember how you used to play Pilgrim's Progress? Nothing delighted you more than to have me tie my piece-bags on your backs for burdens, give you hats and sticks, and rolls of paper, and let you travel through the house from the cellar, which was the City of Destruction, up, up, to the house-top, where you had all the lovely things you could collect to make a Celestial City."

"What fun it was, especially going by the lions, fighting Apollyon, and passing through the Valley where the hobgoblins were," said Jo.

9

"I liked the place where the bundles fell off and tumbled downstairs," said Meg.

"My favourite part was when we came out on the flat roof where our flowers and arbours and pretty things were and all stood and sang for joy up there in the sunshine," said Beth.

"If I wasn't too old for such things, I'd rather like to play it over again," said Amy, who began to talk of renouncing childish things at the mature age of twelve.

"We never are too old for this, my dear, because it is a play we are playing all the time in one way or another. Our burdens are here, our road is before us, and the longing for goodness and happiness is the guide that leads us through many troubles and mistakes to the peace which is a true Celestial City. Now my little pilgrims, suppose you begin again, not in play, but in earnest, and see how far on you can get before father comes home."

"Really, Mother, where are our bundles?" asked Amy.

"Each of you told what your burden was just now except Beth, I rather think she hasn't got any," said her mother.

"Yes, I have; mine is dishes and dusters, and envying girls with nice pianos, and being afraid of people."

Beth's bundle was such a funny one that everybody wanted to laugh; but nobody did, for it would have hurt her feelings very much.

"We were in the Slough of Despond tonight, and mother came and pulled us out, as Help did in the book. We ought to have our roll of directions, like Christian. What shall we do about that?" asked Jo.

"Look under your pillows, Christmas morning, and you will find your guide-book," replied Mrs. March.

## CHAPTER TWO

# A MERRY CHRISTMAS

Jo was the first to wake in the grey dawn of Christmas. No stockings hung at the fireplace, and for a moment she felt disappointment. Then she remembered her mother's promise and slipping her hand under the pillow, drew out a little crimson covered book. She woke Meg with a "Merry Christmas," and bade her see what was under her pillow. A green-coloured book appeared with the same picture inside, and a few words written by their mother, which made their one present very precious. Presently Beth and Amy woke, to rummage and find their little books also — one dove-coloured, the other blue; and all sat looking at and talking about them.

"Girls," said Meg seriously, "mother wants us to read and mind these books, and we must begin at once. I shall keep my book on the table here, and read a little every morning."

Then she opened her new book and began to read. Jo put her arm round her, and leaning cheek to cheek, read also, with the quiet expression so seldom seen on her restless face.

"How good Meg is! Come, Amy, let's do as they do," whispered Beth.

"I'm glad mine is blue," said Amy; and then the rooms were very still while the pages were softly turned, and the winter sunshine crept in to touch the bright heads and serious faces with a Christmas greeting.

"Where is mother?" asked Meg, as she and Jo ran down to thank her for their gifts, half an hour later.

"Goodness only knows. Some poor creeter come a-beggin' and your ma went straight off to see what was needed. There never was such a woman for givin'away wittles and drink, clothes and firin'," replied Hannah, who had lived with the family since Meg was born, and was considered by them all more as a friend than a servant.

"She'll be back soon, I guess; so do your cakes, and have everything ready," said Meg, looking over the presents, which were collected in a basket and kept under the sofa, ready to be produced at the proper time. "Why, where is Amy's bottle of Cologne?" she added, as the little flask did not appear.

"She took it out a minute ago, and went off with it to put a ribbon on it, or some such notion," replied Jo, dancing about the room to take the stiffness off the new army-slippers.

"How nice my handkerchiefs look, don't they? Hannah washed and ironed them for me, and I marked them all myself," said Beth, looking proudly at the somewhat uneven letters which had cost her such labour.

"Bless the child, she's gone and put 'Mother' on them, instead of 'M. March'; how funny!" cried Jo, taking up one.

"Isn't it right? I thought it was better to do so, because Meg's initials are 'M. M.', and I don't want anyone to use these but Marmee," said Beth, looking troubled.

"It's all right, dear, and a very pretty idea; quite sensible, too, for no one can ever mistake now. It will please her very much, I know," said Meg, with a frown for Jo, and a smile for Beth.

"There's mother, hide the basket, quick," said Jo as a door slammed.

Amy came in hastily, and looked rather abashed when she saw her sisters waiting for her.

"Where have you been, and what are you hiding behind you?" asked Meg, surprised to see, by her hood and cloak, that lazy Amy had been out so early.

"Don't laugh at me, Jo; I didn't mean anyone should know till the time came. I only meant to change the little bottle for a big one, and I gave all my money to get it, and I'm not going to be selfish any more."

Another bang of the street door sent the basket under the sofa, and the girls to the table, eager for breakfast.

"Merry Christmas, Marmee! Thank you for our books; we read some, and mean to every day," they cried in chorus.

"Merry Christmas, little daughters! I'm glad you began at once, and hope you will keep on. But I want to say one word before we sit down. Not far away from here lies a poor woman with a little new-born baby. Six children are huddled into one bed to keep them from freezing, for they have no fire. There is nothing to eat over there. My girls, will you give them your breakfast as a Christmas present?"

They were all hungry, having waited nearly an hour, and for a minute no one spoke, only a minute, for Jo exclaimed impetuously, —

"I'm so glad you came before we began!"

"May I go and help carry the things to the poor little children?" asked Beth eagerly.

"I shall take the cream and the muffins," added Amy, giving up the articles she most liked.

Meg was already covering the buckwheats, and piling the bread into one big plate.

"I thought you'd do it," said Mrs. March, smiling, "You shall all go and help me, and when we come back we will have bread and milk for breakfast, and make it up at dinner-time."

They were soon ready, and the procession set out. It was early, and they went through back streets: so few people saw them, and no one laughed at the funny party.

A bare, miserable room it was, with broken windows, no fire, ragged bed-clothes, a sick mother, wailing baby, and a group of pale, hungry children cuddled under one old quilt, trying to keep warm. How the big eyes stared, and the blue lips smiled as the girls went in!

"Ach, mein Gott! It is good angels come to us!" cried the poor woman, crying for joy.

In a few minutes it really did seem as if kind spirits had been at work there. Hannah, who had carried wood, made a fire, and stopped up the broken panes with old hats and her own shawl. Mrs. March gave the mother tea and gruel, and comforted her with promises of help, while she dressed the little baby as tenderly as if it had been her own. The girls meantime spread the table, set the children round the fire, and fed them like so many hungry birds; laughing, talking and trying to understand the funny broken English.

"Der angel-kinder!" cried the poor things, as they ate, and warmed their purple hands at the comfortable blaze. That was a very happy breakfast, though they didn't get any of it; and when they went away, leaving comfort behind, there were not in all the city four merrier people than the hungry little girls who gave away their breakfast on Christmas morning.

"That's loving our neighbour better than ourselves, and I like it," said Meg, as they set out their presents, while their mother was upstairs collecting clothes for the poor Hummels.

Not a very splendid show, but there was a great deal of love done up in the few little bundles; and the tall vase of red roses, white chrysanthemums, and trailing vines, which stood in the middle, gave quite an elegant air to the table.

"She's coming! Strike up, Beth! Open the door, Amy. Three cheers for Marmee!" cried Jo, prancing about, while Meg went to conduct mother to the seat of honour.

Beth played her gayest march, Amy threw open the door, and Meg enacted escort with great dignity. Mrs. March was both surprised and touched; and smiled with her eyes full as she examined her presents, and read the little notes which accompanied them. The slippers went on at once, a new handkerchief was slipped into her pocket, well scented with Amy's Cologne, the rose was fastened in her bosom, and the nice gloves were pronounced "a perfect fit."

The morning charities and ceremonies took so much time that the rest of the day was devoted to preparations for the evening festivities. Being still too young to go often to the theatre, and not rich enough to afford any great outlay for private performances, the girls put their wits to work, and made whatever they needed. Very clever were some of their productions; pasteboard guitars, antique lamps made of old-fashioned butter-boats, covered with silver paper, gorgeous robes of old cotton, glittering with tin spangles from a pickle factory, and armour covered with the same useful diamond-shaped bits.

No gentlemen were admitted; so Jo played male parts to her heart's content and took immense satisfaction in a pair of russet-leather boots given her by a friend. These boots, an old foil, and a slashed doublet, were Jo's chief treasures, and appeared on all occasions. The smallness of the company made it necessary for the two principal actors to take several parts apiece.

On Christmas night, a dozen girls piled on to the bed, which was the dress circle, and sat before the blue and yellow chintz curtains, in a most flattering state of expectancy. There was a good deal of rustling and whispering behind the curtain, a trifle of lamp-smoke, and an occasional giggle from Amy. Presently a bell sounded, the curtains flew apart, and the operatic tragedy began.

"A gloomy wood" was represented by a few shrubs in pots, a green baize on the floor, and a cave in the distance. This cave was made with a clothes-horse for a roof, bureaus for walls; and in it was a small furnace in full blast, with a black pot on it, and an old witch bending over it. Then Hugo, the villain, stalked in with a clanking sword at his side, a slouched hat, black beard, mysterious cloak, and the boots. After pacing to and fro, he struck his forehead, and burst out in a wild strain, singing of his hatred of Roderigo, his love for Zara, and his resolution to kill the one and win the other. The gruff tones of Hugo's voice were very impressive, and the audience applauded the moment he paused for breath. Bowing with the air of one accustomed to public praise, he stole to the cavern, and ordered Hagar to come forth.

Out came Meg, with grey horse-hair hanging about her face, a red and black robe, a staff, and cabalistic signs upon her cloak. Hugo demanded a potion to make Zara adore him and one to destroy Roderigo. Hagar promised both, and proceeded to call up the spirit who would bring the love philtre.

A soft strain of music sounded, and then, at the back of the cave appeared a little figure in cloudy white, with glittering wings, golden hair, and a garland of roses on its head... Waving a wand, and dropping a small bottle at the witch's feet, the spirit vanished. Another chant from Hagar produced another apparition — an ugly black imp appeared, and tossed a dark bottle at Hugo, and disappeared with a mocking laugh. Having warbled his thanks, and put the potions in his boots, Hugo departed; and Hagar informed the audience that, as he had killed a few of her friends in times past, she has cursed him, and intends to thwart his plans, and be revenged on him. Then the curtain fell.

16

A good deal of hammering went on before the curtain rose again. A tower rose to the ceiling; half-way up appeared a window with a lamp burning at it, and behind the white curtain appeared Zara in a lovely blue and silver dress, waiting for Roderigo. He came, in gorgeous array, with plumed cap, red cloak, chestnut love-locks, a guitar, and the boots, of course. Kneeling at the foot of the tower, he sang a serenade. Zara replied, and consented to fly. Roderigo produced a ropeladder, threw up one end, and invited Zara to descend. Timidly she crept from her lattice, put her hand on Roderigo's shoulder, and was about to leap down, when, she forgot her train — it caught in the window; the tower tottered, leaned forward, fell with a crash, and buried the unhappy lovers in the ruins!

A shriek arose as the russet boots waved wildly from the wreck, and a golden head emerged exclaiming. "I told you so!" With wonderful presence of mind, Don Pedro, the cruel sire, rushed in, dragged out his daughter with a hasty aside, — "Don't laugh; act as if it was all right!" and ordering Roderigo up, banished him from the kingdom. Though decidedly shaken by the fall of the tower, Roderigo defied the old gentleman, and refused to stir. This dauntless example fired Zara; she also defied her sire, and he ordered them both to the deepest dungeons of the castle. A stout little retainer came in with chains, and led them away, looking very much frightened, and forgetting the speech he ought to have made.

Act Third, was the castle hall; and here Hagar appeared, having come to free the lovers and finish Hugo. She hears him coming, and hides; sees him put the potions into two cups of wine, and bid the timid little servant "Bear them to the captives in their cells." The servant takes Hugo aside to tell him something, and Hagar changes the cups for two

17

others which are harmless. Ferdinando, the "minion," carries them away, and Hagar puts back the cup which holds the poison meant for Roderigo. Hugo, drinks it, loses his wits, and after a good deal of clutching and stamping, falls flat and dies.

Act Fourth revealed the despairing Roderigo on the point of stabbing himself, because he had been told that Zara has deserted him. Just as the dagger is at his heart, a lovely song is sung under his window, informing him that Zara is true, but in danger. A key is thrown in, which unlocks the door, he tears off his chains, and rushes away to find and rescue his lady-love.

Act Fifth opened with a stormy scene between Zara and Don Pedro. He wishes her to go into a convent, but she won't hear of it; and, is about to faint, when Roderigo dashes in, and demands her hand. Don Pedro refuses, because he is not rich. Roderigo is about to bear away the exhausted Zara when the timid servant enters with a lettler and a bag from Hagar, who has mysteriously disappeared. The letter informs the party that she bequeathes untold wealth to the young pair, and an awful doom to Don Pedro if he doesn't make them happy. The bag is opened, and several quarts of tin money shower down upon the stage. This entirely softens the "stern sire"; all join in a joyful chorus, and the curtain falls upon the lovers kneeling to receive Don Pedro's blessing.

Tumultuous applause followed, but received an unexpected check; for the cot-bed on which the "dress circle" was built suddenly shut up, and extinguished the enthusiastic audience. Roderigo and Don Pedro flew to the rescue, and all were taken out unhurt. The excitement had hardly subsided when Hannah appeared, with "Mrs. March's compliments, and would the ladies walk down to supper."

18

This was a surprise, even to the actors; and when they saw the table they looked at one another in amazement. There was ice-cream — pink and white — and cake, and fruit, and French bonbons, and in the middle of the table four great bouquets of hot-house flowers!

"Is it fairies?" asked Amy.

"It's Santa Claus," said Beth.

"Mother did it," and Meg smiled her sweetest, in spite of her grey beard and white eyebrows.

"Aunt March had a good fit, and sent the supper," cried Jo, with a sudden inspiration.

"All wrong; old Mr. Laurence sent it," replied Mrs. March.

The Laurence boy's grandfather! What in the world put such a thing into his head? We don't know him," exclaimed Meg.

"Hannah told one of his servants about your breakfast party; he is an odd old gentleman, but that pleased him. He knew my father years ago, and he sent me a polite note this afternoon, saying he hoped I would allow him to express his friendly feeling towards my children by sending them a few trifles in honour of the day."

"That boy put it into his head, I know he did! He's a capital fellow, and I wish we could get acquainted. But he's bashful, and Meg is so prim she won't let me speak to him when we pass," said Jo, as the plates went round, and the ice began to melt out of sight.

"You mean the people who live in the big house next door, don't you?" asked one of the girls. "My mother knows old Mr. Laurence, but says he's very proud, and don't like to mix with his neighbours. He keeps his grandson shut up when he isn't riding or walking with his tutor, and makes him study dreadfully hard."

"Our cat ran away once, and he brought her back, an
we talked over the fence, and were getting on capitally
when he saw Meg coming and walked off. I mean to know
him some day, for he needs fun, I'm sure," said Jo decidedly

CHAPTER THREE

# THE LAURENCE BOY

"Jo! Jo! Where are you?" cried Meg, at the foot of th
garret stairs.

"Here," answered a husky voice from above; and runnin
up, Meg found her sister eating apples and crying over th
Heir of Redclyffe, wrapped up in a comforter on an ol
three-legged sofa by the sunny window. This was Jo'
favourite refuge; and here she loved to enjoy the quiet an
the society of a pet rat who lived nearby. As Meg appeared
Scrabble whisked into his hole.

"Such fun! A note of invitation from Mrs. Gardiner fo
tomorrow night!" cried Meg, waving the precious paper, an
then proceeding to read it with delight.

"Mrs. Gardiner would be happy to see Miss March an
Miss Josephine at a little dance on New Year's Eve. Marme
is willing we should go; now what *shall* we wear?"

"What's the use of asking that, when you know we shal
wear our poplins, because we haven't got anything else?"
answered Jo.

"If only I had silk!" sighed Meg.

"I'm sure our pops look like silk, and they are nice enough
for us. Yours is as good as new, but I forgot the burn and
the tear in mine; whatever shall I do?"

"You must sit all you can, and keep your back out of sight; the front is all right. I shall have a new ribbon for my hair, and Marmee will lend me her little pearl pin, and my new slippers are lovely, and my gloves will do."

"Mine are spoilt with lemonade, and I can't get any new ones, so I shall have to go without," said Jo, who never troubled herself much about dress.

"You *must* have gloves, or I won't go," cried Meg decidedly. "You can't dance without them, and if you don't I should be so mortified."

"Then I'll stay still; I don't care much for company dancing."

"You can't ask mother for new ones, they are so expensive. Can't you fix them any way?" asked Meg anxiously.

"No! I'll tell you how we can manage — each wear one good one and carry a bad one."

"Your hands are bigger than mine, and you will stretch my glove dreadfully," began Meg, whose gloves were a tender point with her.

"Then I'll go without. I don't care what people say," cried Jo, taking up her book.

"You may have it, you may! Only don't stain it, and do behave nicely; don't put your hands behind you, or stare, or say 'Christopher Columbus!' will you?"

"Don't worry about me; I'll be as prim as a dish, and not get into any scrapes. Now go and answer your note, and let me finish this story."

So Meg went away to "accept with thanks," look over her dress, and sing blithely as she did up her one real lace frill; while Jo finished her story and her apples.

On New Year's Eve the parlour was deserted, for the two younger girls played dressing-maids, and the two elder were absorbed in the all-important business of "getting ready for the party."

There was a great deal of running up and down, laughing and talking. Meg wanted a few curls about her face, and Jo undertook to pinch the papered locks with a pair of hot tongs.

"Ought they to smoke like that?" asked Beth, from her perch on the bed.

"It's the dampness drying," replied Jo.

"What a queer smell!" observed Amy, smoothing her own pretty curls with a superior air.

"There, now, I'll take off the papers, and you'll see a cloud of little ringlets," said Jo, putting down the tongs.

She did take off the papers, but no cloud of ringlets appeared, for the hair came with the papers, and the horrified hair-dresser laid a row of little scorched bundles on the bureau before her victim.

"Oh, oh, oh! What have you done? I'm spoilt. I can't go! My hair, oh, my hair!" wailed Meg, looking with despair at the uneven frizzle on her forehead.

"Just my luck! You shouldn't have asked me to do it. I'm no end sorry, but the tongs were too hot, and so I've made a mess," groaned poor Jo, regarding the black pancakes with tears of regret.

"It isn't spoilt; just frizzle it, and tie your ribbons so the ends come on your forehead a bit, and it will look like the latest fashion," said Amy consolingly.

After various lesser mishaps, Meg was finished at last, and by the united exertions of the family Jo's hair was got up, and her dress on. They looked very well in their simple suits; Meg in silvery drab, with a blue velvet snood, lace frills, and the pearl pin; Jo in maroon, with a stiff, gentlemanly linen collar, and a white chrysanthemum or two for her only ornament. Each put on one nice white glove, and carried one soiled on. Meg's high-heeled slippers were dreadfully tight, though she would not own it; and Jo's nineteen hairpins all seemed stuck straight into the head, but, dear me, let us be elegant or die.

"Have a good time, dearies," said Mrs. March, as the sisters went daintily down the walk. "Don't eat much supper, and come away at eleven, when I send Hannah for you." As the gate clashed behind them, a voice cried from a window, — "Girls, girls!" *have* you both got nice pocket handkerchiefs ?"

"Yes, yes, and Meg has Cologne on hers," cried Jo; adding, with a laugh, "I do believe Marmee would ask that if we were all running away from an earthquake."

"Now don't forget to keep the bad breadth out of sight Jo. Is my sash right; and does my hair look *very* bad?" said Meg, as she turned from the glass in Mrs. Gardiner's dressing-room.

"I know I shall forget. If you see me doing anything wrong, you just remind me by a wink, will you?" returned Jo.

"No, winking isn't lady-like; I'll lift my eyebrows if anything is wrong, and nod if you are all right. Now hold your shoulders straight, and take short steps."

Down they went, feeling a trifle timid. Mrs. Gardiner, a stately old lady, greeted them kindly and handed them over to the eldest of her six daughters. Meg knew Sallie, and was at her ease very soon; but Jo, who didn't care much for girlish gossip, stood about with her back carefully against the wall, and felt as much out of place as a colt in a flower-garden. Half a dozen jovial lads were talking about skates in another part of the room, and she longed to go and join them. She telegraphed her wishes to Meg, but the eyebrows went up so alarmingly that she dared not stir. She could not roam about and amuse herself, for the burnt breadth would show; so she stared at people rather forlornly till the dancing began.

Jo saw a red-headed youth approaching her corner, and fearing he meant to engage her, she slipped into a curtained recess. Unfortunately, another bashful person had chosen the same refuge; for, as the curtain fell behind her, she found herself face to face with the "Laurence boy."

"Dear me, I didn't know anyone was here," stammered Jo.

But the boy laughed, and said pleasantly. "Don't mind me; stay if you like."

"Shan't I disturb you?"

"Not a bit; I only came here because I don't know many people."

"So did I. Don't go away, please, unless you'd rather."

The boy sat down again and looked at his boots, till Jo said, trying to be polite and easy. "I think I've had the pleasure of seeing you before. You live near us, don't you?"

"Next door"; and he looked up and laughed outright; for Jo's prim manner was rather funny when he remembered how they had chatted when he brought the cat home.

That put Jo at her ease; and she laughed too, as she said, in her heartiest way, "We did have such a good time over your nice Christmas present."

"Grandpa sent it."

"But you put it into his head, didn't you, now?"

"How is your cat, Miss March?" asked the boy, trying to look sober, while his black eyes shone with fun.

"Nicely, thank you, Mr. Laurence; but I ain't Miss March, I'm only Jo."

"I'm not Mr. Laurence, I'm only Laurie. Don't you like to dance, Miss Jo?" asked Laurie.

"I like it well enough if there is plenty of room. In a place like this I'm sure to upset something, tread on people's toes, or do something dreadful; so I keep out of mischief, and let Meg do the pretty. Don't you dance?"

"Sometimes. You see, I've been abroad a good many years, and haven't been about enough yet to know how you do things here."

"Abroad!" cried Jo; "oh tell me about it!" Jo's eager questions soon set him going; and he told her how he had been at school at Vevey, where the boys had a fleet of boats on the lake, and for holiday fun went walking trips about Switzerland with their teachers.

"Don't I wish I'd been there!" cried Jo. "Did you go to Paris ?"

"We spent last winter there."

"Can you talk French?"

"We were not allowed to speak anything else at Vevey."

"Do say some. I can read it, but can't pronounce."

"Quel nom a cette jeune demoiselle en les pantoufles jolies?" said Laurie good-naturedly.

"How nicely you do it! Let me see — you said, 'Who is the young lady in the pretty slippers?"

"Oui, mademoiselle.'"

"It's my sister Margaret, and you knew it was! Do you think she is pretty?"

"Yes; she makes me think of the German girls, she looks so fresh and quiet, and dances like a lady."

Jo quite glowed with pleasure at this boyish praise of her sister. Laurie's bashfulness soon wore off, for Jo's gentlemanly demeanour amused and set him at his ease, and Jo was her merry self again, because her dress was forgotten, and nobody lifted her eyebrows at her. She liked the "Laurence boy" better than ever, and took several good looks at him, so that she might describe him to the girls.

"I suppose you are going to college soon? I see you are pegging away at your books — no, I mean studying hard"; and Jo blushed at the dreadful "pegging" which had escaped her.

Laurie smiled, but didn't seem shocked, and answered with a shrug, "not for two or three years yet; I won't go before seventeen, anyway."

"How I wish I was going to college; you don't look as if you liked it."

"I hate it; nothing but grinding or sky-larking; and I don't like the way fellows do either in this country."

"What do you like?"

"To live in Italy, and to enjoy myself in my own way."

Jo wanted to ask what his own way was; but his black brows looked rather threatening as he knit them, so she changed the subject by saying, "That's a splendid polka; why don't you go and try it?"

"If you come too," he answered with a queer little French bow.

"I can't; for I told Meg I wouldn't because — "There Jo stopped, and looked undecided whether to tell or to laugh.

"Because what?" asked Laurie curiously.

"You won't tell?"

"Never!"

"Well, I have a bad trick of standing before the fire, and so I burn my frocks, and I scorched this one; and though it's nicely mended, it shows, and Meg told me to keep still, so no one would see it. You may laugh if you want to."

But Laurie didn't laugh; he only looked down a minute, and the expression on his face puzzled Jo; when he said very gently, "Never mind that; I'll tell you how we can manage: there's a long hall out there, and we can dance grandly, and no one will see us. Please come."

Jo thanked him, and gladly went, and wishing she had two neat gloves when she saw the nice pearl-coloured ones her partner put on. The hall was empty, and they had a grand polka, for Laurie danced well. When the music stopped they sat down on the stairs to get their breath, and Laurie was in the midst of an account of a students' festival at Heidelberg, when Meg appeared in search of her sister. She beckoned, and Jo followed her into a side-room, where she found her on a sofa holding her foot, and looking pale.

"I've sprained my ankle. That stupid high heel turned, and gave me a horrid wrench. It aches so, I can hardly stand."

"I knew you'd hurt your feet with those silly things I'm sorry; but I don't see what you can do, except get a carriage, or stay here all night," answered Jo, softly rubbing the poor ankle as she spoke. "I can't have a carriage without its cósting ever so much; I dare say I can't get one at all, for most people come in their own, and it's a long way to the stable, and no one to send."

"I'll go."

"No, indeed; it's past ten, and dark as Egypt. I can't stop here, for the house is full; Sallie has some girls staying with her. I'll rest till Hannah comes, and then do the best I can."

"I'll ask Laurie; he will go," said Jo.

"Mercy, no! Don't ask or tell anyone. Get me my rubbers, and put these slippers with our things. I can't dance any more; but as soon as supper is over, watch for Hannah, and tell me the minute she comes."

"They are going out to supper now. I'll stay with you; I'd rather."

"No, dear; run along, and bring me some coffee. I'm so tired, I can't stir."

So Meg reclined, with the rubbers well hidden, and Jo went blundering away to the dining-room, which she found after going into a china closet and opening the door of a room where old Mr. Gardiner was taking a little private refreshment. Making a dive at the table, she secured the coffee, which she immediately spilt, thereby making the front of her dress as bad as the back.

"Can I help you?" said a friendly voice; and there was Laurie, with a full cup in one hand and a plate of ice in the other.

"I was trying to get something for Meg, who is very tired, and someone shook me, and here I am, in a nice state," answered Jo.

"Too bad! I was looking for someone to give this to; may I take it to your sister?"

"Oh, thank you; I'll show you where she is." Jo led the way, and Laurie drew up a little table, brought a second instalment of coffee and ice for Jo, was so obliging that Meg pronounced him a "nice boy." They had a merry time over the bonbons and mottoes and were in the midst of a quiet game of "buzz" with two or three other young people who had strayed in, when Hannah appeared. Meg forgot her foot, and rose so quickly that she was forced to catch hold of Jo, with an exclamation of pain.

"Hush! don't say anything," she whispered; adding aloud, "It's nothing; I turned my foot a little — that's all," and limped upstairs to put her things on.

Hannah scolded, Meg cried, and Jo was at her wits' end, till she decided to take things into her own hands. Slipping out, she ran down, and was looking round for help, when Laurie came up and offered his grandfather's carriage.

"It's so early, — you can't mean to go yet," began Jo, looking relieved.

"I always go early — I do, truly. Please let me take you home; it's all on my way, you know, and it rains, they say."

That settled it; and, telling him of Meg's mishap, Jo gratefully accepted and rushed up to bring down the rest of the party. Hannah hated rain as much as a cat does; so she made no trouble, and they rolled away in the luxurious carriage, feeling very festive and elegant. Laurie went on the box, so Meg could keep her foot up, and the girls talked over their party in freedom.

"I had a capital time; did you?" asked Jo, rumpling up her hair.

"Yes, till I hurt myself. Sallie's friend, Annie Moffat, took a fancy to me, and asked me to come and spend a week with her when Sallie does. She is going in the spring, when the Opera comes, and it will be perfectly splendid if mother only lets me go," answered Meg, cheering up at the thought.

Jo told her adventures, and by the time she had finished they were at home. With many thanks, they said, "Good night," and crept in, hoping to disturb no one; but the instant their door creaked, two little night-caps bobbed up, and two sleepy voices cried out — "Tell about the party!"

With what Meg called "a great want of manners," Jo had saved some bonbons for the little girls, and they soon subsided, after hearing the most thrilling events of the evening.

"I declare, it really seems like being a fine young lady, to come home from my party in my carriage, and sit in my dressing-gown, with a maid to wait on me," said Meg, as Jo bound up her foot, and brushed her hair.

"I don't believe fine young ladies enjoy themselves a bit more than we do, in spite of our burnt hair, old gowns, one glove apiece, and tight slippers that sprain our ankles when we are silly enough to wear them."

## CHAPTER FOUR

# BURDENS

"Oh dear, how hard it does seem to take up our packs," sighed Meg, the morning after the party.

"I wish it was Christmas or New Year all the time; wouldn't it be fun?" answered Jo, yawning dismally.

"We shouldn't enjoy ourselves half so much as we do now. But it does seem so nice to have little suppers and bouquets, and go to parties. It's like other people, you know, and I always envy girls who do such things; I'm so fond of luxury," said Meg.

"Well, we can't have it; so don't let's grumble, but shoulder our bundles and trudge along as cheerfully as Marmee does. I'm sure Aunt March is a regular Old Man of the Sea to me, but I suppose when I've learned to carry her without complaining she will tumble off."

This idea tickled Jo's fancy, and put her in good spirits; but Meg didn't brighten, for her burden, consisting of four spoilt children, seemed heavier than ever. She hadn't heart enough even to make herself pretty, as usual, by putting on a blue neck ribbon.

"Where's the use of looking nice when no one sees me but those cross fidgets," she muttered.

So Meg went down, wearing an injured look. Everyone seemed rather out of sorts, and inclined to croak. Beth had a headache, and lay on the sofa trying to comfort herself with the cat and three kittens; Amy was fretting because her lessons were not learned and she couldn't find her rubbers; Jo would whistle, and make a great racket getting ready. Mrs. March was very busy trying to finish a letter, which must go at once and Hannah had the grumps, for being late didn't suit her.

"Girls! Girls! Do be quiet one moment. I must get this off by the early mail," cried Mrs. March.

There was a lull, broken by Hannah, who bounced in, laid two hot turnovers on the table, and bounced out again. These turnovers were an institution; and the girls called them "muffs" for they had no others, and found the hot pies very comforting to their hands on cold mornings. Hannah never forgot to make them, no matter how busy or grumpy she might be, for the walk was long and bleak; the poor things got no other lunch and were seldom home before three.

"Cuddle your cats, and get over your headache, Bethy. Good-bye, Marmee; we are a set of rascals this morning, but we'll come home regular angels. Now, then, Meg"; and Jo tramped away, feeling that the pilgrims were not setting out as they ought to do.

They always looked back before turning the corner, for their mother was always at the window, to nod, and smile, and wave her hand to them.

When Mr. March lost his property in trying to help an unfortunate friend, the two eldest girls begged to be allowed to do something towards their own support. Margaret found a place as nursery governess. As she said, she was "fond of luxury," and her chief trouble was poverty. She found it harder to bear than the others, because she could remember a time when want of any kind was unknown. At the Kings' she daily saw all she wanted, for the children's older sisters were just out, and Meg caught glimpses of dainty ball-dresses and bouquets, heard lively gossip about theatres, and merry-makings of all kinds.

Jo happened to suit Aunt March, who was lame, and needed an active person to wait upon her. The childless old lady had offered to adopt one of the girls when the troubles came, and was much offended because her offer was declined.

Other friends told the Marches that they had lost all chance of being remembered in the rich old lady's will; but the unwordly Marches only said, "We can't give up our girls for a dozen fortunes."

The old lady wouldn't speak to them for a time, but happened to meet Jo at a friend's, something in her comical face and blunt manners struck the old lady's fancy, and she proposed to take her for a companion. This did not suit Jo at all; but she accepted the place, since nothing better appeared, and, to everyone's surprise, got on remarkably well with her irascible relative.

I suspect that the real attraction was a large library of fine books, which was left to dust and spiders since Uncle March died.

The moment Aunt March took her nap or was busy with company, Jo hurried to this quiet place, and devoured poetry, romance, history, travels, and pictures, like a regular bookworm. But like all happiness, it did not last long; a shrill voice called "Josephine! Josephine!" and she had to leave her paradise to wind yarn, wash the poodle, or read Belsham's Essays.

Jo's ambition was to do something very splendid; and, meanwhile, she found her greatest affliction in the fact that she couldn't read, run, and ride as much as she liked. A quick temper, sharp tongue, and restless spirit were always getting her into scrapes, and her life was a series of ups and downs. But the training she received at Aunt March's was just what she needed; and the thought that she was doing something to support herself made her happy, in spite of the perpetual "Josephine!"

Beth was too bashful to go to school, and she did her lessons at home, with her father. Even when he went away, and her mother was called to devote her energy to Soldiers'

Aid Societies, Beth went faithfully on by herself. She was a housewifely little creature, and helped Hannah keep home neat and comfortable for the workers. Her little world was peopled with imaginary friends. There were six dolls to be taken up and dressed every morning; not one whole or handsome one among them; for, when her sisters outgrew these idols, they passed to her. One forlorn fragment of dollanity had belonged to Jo; and having led a tempestuous life, was left a wreck in the rag-bag, from which dreary poor-house it was rescued by Beth. Having no top to its head, she tied on a little neat cap, and, as both arms and legs were gone, she hid these deficiencies by folding it in a blanket, and devoting her best bed to this chronic invalid. She brought it bits of bouquets; she read to it, took it out to breathe the air, she sang it lullabys, and never went to bed without kissing its dirty face, and whispering tenderly, "I hope you'll have a good night, my poor dear."

Beth had her troubles as well as the others; and often "Wept a little weep," because she couldn't take music lessons and have a fine piano. She loved music so dearly, tried so hard to learn and practised away so patiently at the jingling old instrument.

If anyone had asked Amy what the greatest trial of her life was she would have answered, "My nose." When she was a baby, Jo had accidentally dropped her into the coal-hod, and Amy insisted that the fall had ruined her nose for ever. It was not big, nor red; it was only rather flat, and all the pinching in the world could not give it an aristocratic point. No one minded it but herself, and it was doing its best to grow, but Amy felt deeply the want of a Grecian nose, and drew whole sheets of handsome ones to console herself.

"Little Raphael," as her sisters called her, had a decided talent for drawing, and was never so happy as when copying flowers, designing fairies, or illustrating stories. Her teachers complained that, instead of doing her sums, she covered her slate with animals. She got through her lessons as well as she could, and managed to escape reprimands by being a model of deportment. Her little airs and graces were much admired, so were her accomplishments; for, besides her drawing, she could play twelve tunes, crochet, and read French without mispronouncing more than two-thirds of the words.

Amy was in a fair way to be spoilt; for everyone petted her. One thing, however, rather quenched her vanities; she had to wear her cousin's clothes. Now Florence's mamma hadn't a particle of taste, and Amy suffered deeply at having to wear a red instead of a blue bonnet, unbecoming gowns, and fussy aprons.

Meg was Amy's confidante and monitor, and, by some strange attraction of opposites, Jo was gentle Beth's. To Jo alone did the shy girl tell her thoughts; and over her big harum-scarum sister Beth exercised more influence than anyone in her family. The two older girls were a great deal to each other, but both took one of the younger into their keeping, "playing mother" they called it, and put their sisters in the place of discarded dolls.

"Has anybody got anything to tell? It's been such a dismal day, I'm really dying for some amusement," said Meg, as they sat sewing together that evening.

"I had a queer time with aunt today," began Jo, who dearly loved to tell stories. "I was reading that everlasting Belsham, and droning away as I always do, for aunt soon drops off, and then I take out some nice book, and read like fury, till she wakes up. I actually made myself sleepy; and, before she began to nod, I gave such a gape that she asked me what I meant by opening my mouth wide enough to take the whole book in at once."

"'I wish I could, and be done with it,' said I."

"Then she gave me a long lecture on my sins, and told me to sit and think over them while she just 'lost' herself for a moment. She never finds herself very soon; so the minute her cap began to bob, I whipped the Vicar of Wakefield out of my pocket. I'd just got to where they all tumbled into the water, when I forgot and laughed out loud. Aunt woke up; and, being good-natured after her nap, told me to read a bit. I did my best, and she liked it, though she only said, 'I don't understand what it's all about; go back and begin it, child'."

"Back I went, and made the Primroses as interesting as I could. Once I was wicked enough to stop in a thrilling place, and say meekly, 'I'm afraid it tired you. ma'am; shan't I stop now?'"

"She caught up her knitting, gave me a sharp look through her specs, and said in her short way, 'Finish the chapter, and don't be impertinent, miss.'"

"Did she own she liked it?" asked Meg.

"Oh, bless you, no! But she let old Belsham rest; and, when I ran back after my gloves this afternoon, there she was, so hard at the Vicar, that she did not hear me laugh as I danced a jig in the hall."

"That reminds me," said Meg, "that I've got something to tell. At the Kings' today, I found everybody in a flurry, and one of the children said that her oldest brother had done something dreadful, and papa had sent him away. I heard Mrs. King crying and Mr. King talking very loud, and Grace and Ellen turned away their faces when they passed me. I felt so sorry for them, and was rather glad I hadn't any wild brothers to do wicked things and disgrace the family."

"I think being disgraced in school is a great deal tryinger than anything bad boys can do," said Amy. "Susie Perkins came to school today with a lovely red carnelian ring; I wanted it dreadfully, and wished I was her with all my might. Well, she drew a picture of Mr. Davis, with a monstrous nose and a hump, and the words, 'Young ladies, my eye is upon you!' coming out of his mouth in a balloon thing. We were laughing over it, when all at once his eye *was* on us, and he ordered Susie to bring up her slate. She was paralysed with fright, but she went: and, oh, what *do* you think he did? He took her by the ear, the ear! and led her to the recitation platform, and made her stand there half an hour, holding that slate so everyone could see."

"I saw something that I liked this morning," said Beth. "When I went to get some oysters for Hannah, Mr. Laurence was in the fish shop. A poor woman came in with a pail and a mop, and asked Mr. Cutter if he would let her do some scrubbing for a bit of fish, because she hadn't any dinner for her children. Mr. Cutter was in a hurry, and said 'No', rather crossly; so she was going away, when Mr. Laurence hooked up a big fish with the crooked end of his cane, and held it out to her. She was so glad she took it right in her arms, and thanked him over and over. Oh, she did look so funny, hugging the big slippery fish, and hoping Mr. Laurence's bed in heaven would be 'airy'."

When they had laughed at Beth's story, they asked their mother for one; and, she said soberly, 'As I sat cutting out blue flannel jackets today, at the rooms, I felt anxious about father. I kept on worrying, till an old man came in with an order for some things. He sat down near me, and I began to talk to him.

"'Have you sons in the army?' I asked.

"'Yes, Ma'am; I had four, but two were killed; one is a prisoner, and I'm going to the other, who is very sick in a Washington hospital.'

"'You have done a great deal for your country, sir,' I said, feeling respect now, instead of pity.

"'Not a mite more than I ought, Ma'am, I'd go myself, if I was any use; as I ain't, I give my boys, and give 'em free.'

"He spoke so cheerfully, looked so sincere, and seemed so glad to give his all, that I was ashamed of myself; I felt so rich, so happy, thinking of my blessings, that I made him a nice bundle, gave him some money, and thanked him heartily for the lesson he had taught me."

"Tell me another story, mother; one with a moral to it, like this. I like to think about them afterwards, if they are real, and not too preachy," said Jo.

Mrs. March smiled, and began at once.

"Once upon a time there were four girls, who had enough to eat, and drink, and wear, kind friends and parents, who loved them dearly, and yet they were not contented." (Here the listeners stole sly looks at one another, and began to sew diligently.) "These girls were anxious to be good, and made many resolutions, but somehow they did not keep them very well, and were constantly saying, 'If we only had this,' or, 'If we could only do that,' forgetting how much they already had; so they asked an old woman what spell they could use to make them happy, and she said, 'When you feel discontented, think over your blessings, and be grateful.'

"They decided to try her advice, and were surprised to see how well off they were. One discovered that money couldn't keep shame and sorrow out of rich people's houses; another, that, though she was poor, she was a great deal happier with her youth and good spirits than a certain fretful old lady, who couldn't enjoy her comforts; a third, that, disagreeable as it was to help get dinner, it was harder still to have to go begging for it; and the fourth, that even carnelian rings were not so valuable as good behaviour. So they agreed to stop complaining, to enjoy the blessings already possessed, and try to deserve them, lest they should be taken away entirely, instead of increased."

"Now, Marmee, that is very cunning of you to turn our stories against us."

"I like that kind of sermon; it's the sort father used to tell us," said Beth thoughtfully.

"We needed that lesson, and we won't forget it. If we do, you just say to us as Old Chole did in *Uncle Tom* — 'Tink ob yer marcies, chillen, tink ob yer marcies,' " added Jo, who could not for the life of her help getting a morsel of fun.

CHAPTER FIVE

# BEING NEIGHBOURLY

"What in the world are you going to do now, Jo?" asked Meg, one snowy afternoon, as her sister came clumping through the hall, in rubber boots, old sack and hood, with a broom in one hand and a shovel in the other.

"Going out for exercise," answered Jo, with a mischievous twinkle in her eyes.

Meg went back to toast her feet, and read *Ivanhoe*, and Jo began to dig paths with great energy. The snow was light; and her broom soon swept a path all round the garden, for Beth to walk in when the sun came out, and the invalid dolls needed air. Now the garden separated the Marches' house from that of Mr. Laurence; both stood in a suburb of the city. A low hedge parted the two estates. On one side was a stately stone mansion plainly betokening every sort of comfort and luxury, from the big coach-house and well-kept grounds to the conservatory, and the glimpses of lovely things one caught between the rich curtains. Yet it seemed a lonely lifeless sort of house; for no children frolicked on the lawn, no motherly face ever smiled at the windows, and few people went in and out, except the old gentleman and his grandson.

To Jo's lively fancy this fine house seemed a kind of enchanted palace, full of splendours and delights. She had long wanted to behold these hidden glories, and to know the "Laurence boy," who looked as if he would like to be known. Since the party, she had planned many ways of making friends with him; but he had not been lately seen, and Jo began to think he had gone away, when she one day spied a brown face at an upper window, looking wistfully down into their garden, where Beth and Amy were snowballing one another.

"That boy is suffering for society and fun," she said to herself. "His grandpa don't know what's good for him, and keeps him shut up all alone. I've a great mind to go over and tell the old gentleman so."

The idea amused Jo, who liked do to daring things. The plan of "going over" was not forgotten; and when the snowy afternoon came, Jo resolved to try what could be done. She saw Mr. Laurence drive off, and then sallied out to dig her way down to the hedge, where she paused, and took a survey. All quiet; curtains drawn at the lower windows; servants out of sight, and nothing human visible but a curly black head leaning on a thin hand, at the upper window.

Up went a handful of soft snow, and the head turned at once, showing a face which lost its listless look in a minute, as the big eyes brightened and the mouth began to smile. Jo nodded, and laughed, and flourished her broom as she called out, "How do you do? Are you sick?"

Laurie opened the window and croaked out as hoarsely as a raven, "better, thank you. I've had a horrid cold, and been shut up for a week."

"What do you amuse yourself with?"

"Nothing."

"Isn't there some nice girl who'd read and amuse you?"

"Don't know any."

"You know me," began Jo.

"So I do! Will you come, please?" cried Laurie.

"I'm not quiet and nice; but I'll come, if mother will let me. I'll go and ask her. Shut the window like a good boy, and wait till I come."

With that Jo shouldered her broom and marched into the house. Laurie was in a flutter of excitement at the idea of having company, and flew about to get ready, and did honour to the coming guest by brushing his curly pate, putting on a fresh collar, and trying to tidy up the room. Presently there came a loud ring, then a decided voice, asking for "Mr. Laurie," and a surprised-looking servant came running up to announce a young lady.

"All right, show her up; it's Miss Jo," said Laurie, going to the door of his little parlour to meet Jo, who appeared, looking rosy and kind, with a covered dish in one hand and Beth's three kittens in the other.

"Here I am, bag and baggage," she said briskly. "Mother sent her love. Meg wanted me to bring some of her blanc-mange; and Beth thought her cats would be comforting."

It so happened that Beth's funny loan was just the thing; for, in laughing over the kits, Laurie forgot his bashfulness, and grew sociable at once.

"That looks too pretty to eat," he said, smiling with pleasure as Jo uncovered the dish and showed the blanc-mange, surrounded by a garland of green leaves and the scarlet flowers of Amy's pet geranium.

"Tell the girl to put it away for your tea; being soft, it will slip down without hurting your sore throat. What a cosy room this is!"

"It might be, if it was kept nice; but the maids are lazy."

"I'll right it up in two minutes; for it only needs to have the hearth brushes, so — and the things stood straight on the mantlepiece, so — and the books put here, and the bottles there, and your sofa turned from the light, and the pillows plumped up a bit. Now, then, you're fixed."

And so he was; for, as she laughed and talked, Jo had whisked things into place, and given quite a different air to the room. Laurie watched her in respectful silence; and, when she beckoned him on his sofa, he sat down, saying gratefully, "How kind you are! Now take the big chair, and let me do something to amuse my company."

"No; I came to amuse you. Shall I read aloud?"

"If you don't mind, I'd rather talk," answered Laurie.

"Not a bit; I'll talk all day if you'll only set me going. Beth says I never know when to stop."

"Is Beth the rosy one, who stays at home a good deal, and sometimes goes out with a little basket?" asked Laurie with interest.

"Yes, that's Beth; she's my girl, and a regular good one she is too."

"The pretty one is Meg, and the curly-haired one is Amy, I believe?"

"How did you find that out?"

Laurie coloured up, but answered frankly, "Why, you see, I often hear you calling to one another, and when I'm alone up here, I can't help looking over at your house, you always seem to be having such good times. Sometimes you forget to put down the curtain at the window where the flowers are; and, when the lamps are lighted, it's like looking at a picture to see the fire, and you all round the table with your mother; her face is right opposite, and it looks so sweet behind the flowers, I can't help watching it. I haven't got any mother, you know"; and Laurie poked the fire to hide a little twitching of the lips.

The solitary hungry look in his eyes went straight to Jo's warm heart. Her face was very friendly, as she said, "we'll never draw that curtain any more. I just wish, though, instead of peeping, you'd come over and see us. Mother is so splendid, she'd do you heaps of good, and Beth would sing to you if I begged her to, and Amy would dance; Meg and I would make you laugh over our funny stage properties, and we'd have jolly times. Wouldn't your grandpa let you?"

"I think he would, if your mother asked him. He's very kind, though he don't look it; and he lets me do what I like pretty much, only he's afraid I might be a bother to strangers," began Laurie, brightening more and more. "You see, grandpa lives among his books, and don't mind much what happens outside. Mr. Brooke, my tutor, don't stay here, and I have no one to go round with me, so I just stop at home."

"That's bad; you ought to make a dive, and go visiting everywhere you are asked."

"Do you like your school?" asked the boy, after a little pause.

"Don't go to school; I'm a business man — girl, I mean. I go to wait on my aunt, and a dear, cross old soul she is too," answered Jo.

She gave him a lively description of the fidgety old lady, the parrot that talked Spanish, and the library where she revelled. Laurie enjoyed that immensely; and when she told about the prim old gentleman who came once to woo Aunt March, and, in the middle of a fine speech, how Poll had tweaked his wig off, the boy lay back and laughed till the tears ran down his cheeks, and a maid popped her head in to see what was the matter.

"Oh! that does me lots of good; tell on, please," he said, taking his face out of the sofa-cushion, red and shining with merriment.

Much elated with her success, Jo did "tell on," all about their plays and plans, their hopes and fears for father, and the most interesting events of the little world in which the sisters lived. Then they got to talking about books; and to Jo's delight she found that Laurie loved them as well as she did.

"If you like them so much, come down and see ours, Grandpa is out, so you needn't be afraid," said Laurie, getting up.

"I'm not afraid of anything," returned Jo.

"I don't believe you are!" exclaimed the boy, looking up at her with much admiration. Laurie led the way from room to room, letting Jo stop to examine whatever struck her fancy; and so at last they came to the library. It was lined with books, and there were pictures and statues, and distracting little cabinets full of coins and curiosities, and Sleepy-Hollow chairs, and queer tables and bronzes.

"What richness!" sighed Jo, sinking into the depths of a velvet chair. "Theodore Laurence, you ought to be the happiest boy in the world."

"A fellow can't live on books," said Laurie.

Before he could say any more a bell rang, and Jo flew up, exclaiming with alarm, "Mercy me! it's your grandpa."

"Well, what if it is? You are not afraid of anything," returned the boy, looking wicked.

"I think I am a little afraid of him, but I don't know why I should be. Marmee said I might come, and I don't know why you'd be any the worse for it," said Jo.

"I'm a great deal better for it."

"The doctor to see you, sir," and the maid beckoned as she spoke.

"Would you mind if I left you for a minute?" said Laurie.

"Don't mind me. I'm as happy as a cricket here," answered Jo.

Laurie went away, and his guest amused herself in her own way. She was standing before a fine portrait of the old gentleman when the door opened again, and, without turning, she said decidedly, "I'm sure now that I shouldn't be afraid of him, for he's got kind eyes, though his mouth is grim, and he looks as if he had a will of his own. He isn't as handsome as *my* grandfather, but I like him."

"Thank you, ma'am," said a gruff voice behind her; and there, to her great dismay, stood old Mr. Laurence.

Poor Jo blushed till she couldn't blush any redder. For a minute a wild desire to run away possessed her; but that was cowardly; so she resolved to stay, and get out of the scrape as she could. A second look showed her that the living eyes, under the bushy grey eyebrows, were kinder even than the painted ones; and there was a sly twinkle in them. The gruff voice was gruffer than ever, as the old gentleman said abruptly, "So you're not afraid of me, hey?"

"Not much, sir."

"And you don't think me as handsome as your grandfather?"

"Not quite, sir."

"But you like me in spite of it?"

"Yes, I do, sir."

That answer pleased the old gentleman; he gave a short laugh, shook hands with her, and turned up her face, examined it gravely, and let it go, saying, with a nod, "You've got your grandfather's spirit, if you haven't his face."

"Thank you, sir."

"What have you been doing to this boy of mine, hey?"

"Only trying to be neighbourly, sir," and Jo told how her visit came about.

"You think he needs cheering up a bit, do you?"

"Yes, sir; he seems a little lonely, and young folks would do him good, perhaps. We are only girls, but we should be glad to help if we could, for we don't forget the splendid Christmas present you sent us," said Jo eagerly.

"Tut, tut, tut; that was my boy's affair. How is the poor woman?"

"Doing nicely, sir" and off went Jo, talking very fast, as she told about the Hummels.

"I shall come and see your mother some fine day. There's the tea-bell. Come down, and go on being neighbourly."

"If you'd like to have me, sir."

"Shouldn't ask you if I didn't," said Mr. Laurence offering his arm with old-fashioned courtesy.

Laurie came running downstairs, and brought up with a start of surprise at the astonishing sight of Jo arm-in-arm with the redoubtable grandfather.

"I didn't know you'd come, sir," he began, as Jo gave him a triumphant little glance.

"That's evident by the way you racket downstairs. Come to your tea, sir, and behave like a gentleman"; and having pulled the boy's hair by way of a caress, Mr. Laurence walked on, while Laurie went through a series of comic evolutions behind their backs, which nearly produced an explosion of laughter from Jo.

The old gentleman did not say much as he drank his four cups of tea, but he watched the young people, who soon chatted away like old friends, and the change in his grandson did not escape him. There was colour, light and life in the boy's face now, vivacity in his manner, and genuine merriment in his laugh.

"She's right; the lad is lonely. I'll see what those little girls can do for him," thought Mr. Laurence, as he looked and listened. He liked Jo, for her odd, blunt ways suited him; and she seemed to understand the boy as well as if she had been one herself.

When they rose, she proposed to go, but Laurie said he had something more to show her, and took her away to the conservatory; It seemed quite fairy-like to Jo, as she went up and down the walks, while her new friend cut the finest flowers till his hands were full; then he tied them up, saying, "Please give these to your mother, and tell her I like the medicine she sent me very much."

They found Mr. Laurence standing before the fire in the great drawing-room, but Jo's attention was absorbed by a grand piano, which stood open.

"Do you play?" she asked, turning to Laurie.

"Sometimes," he answered modestly.

"Please do now; I want to hear it, so I can tell Beth."

So Laurie played, and Jo listened, with her nose luxuriously buried in heliotrope and tea roses. Her respect and regard for the "Laurence boy" increased. For he played remarkably well, and didn't put on any airs. She wished Beth could hear him but she did not say so; only praised him till he was quite abashed, and his grandfather came to the rescue. "That will do, young lady; too many sugar-plums are not good for him. His music isn't bad, but I hope he will do as well in more important things. Going? Well, I'm much obliged to you, and I hope you'll come again. My respects to your mother."

He shook hands kindly, but looked as if something did not please him. When they got into the hall, Jo asked Laurie if she had said anything amiss.

"No; it was me: he don't like to hear me play."

"Why not?"

"I'll tell you some day. John is going home with you, as I can't."

"No need of that; I ain't a young lady, and it's only a step. Take care of yourself, won't you?"

"Yes, but you will come again, I hope?"

"If you promise to come and see us after you are well."

"I will."

"Good night, Laurie!"

"Good night, Jo; good night!"

When all the afternoon's adventures had been told, the family felt inclined to go visiting in a body, for each found something very attractive in the big house on the other side of the hedge. Mrs. March wanted to talk of her father with the old man who had not forgotten him; Meg longed to walk in the conservatory; Beth sighed for the grand piano; and Amy was eager to see the fine pictures and statues.

"Mother, why didn't Mr. Laurence like to have Laurie play?" asked Jo.

"I think it was because his son, Laurie's father, married an Italian lady, a musician, which displeased the old man. The lady was good and lovely, but he did not like her, and never saw his son after he married. They both died when Laurie was a little child, and then his grandfather took him home. I fancy the boy, who was born in Italy, is not very strong, and the old man is afraid of losing him. Laurie comes naturally by his love of music, for he is like his mother, and

I dare say his grandfather fears that he may want to be a musician; at any rate, his skill reminds him of the woman he did not like."

"How silly!" said Jo; "let him be a musician if he wants to, and not plague his life out sending him to college, when he hates to go."

"That's why he has such handsome black eyes and pretty manners, I suppose; Italians are always nice," said Meg; she was a little sentimental. "That was a nice little speech about the medicine mother sent him."

"He meant the blanc-mange, I suppose."

"How stupid you are, child! he meant you, of course."

"Did he?" and Jo opened her eyes as if it had never occurred to her before.

"I never saw such a girl! You don't know a compliment when you get it," said Meg.

"I think they are great nonsense, and I'll thank you not to be silly, and spoil my fun. Laurie's a nice boy, and I like him, and I won't have any sentimental stuff about compliments. We'll all be good to him because he hasn't any mother, and he may come over and see us, mayn't he, Marmee?"

"Yes, Jo, your little friend is very welcome; and I hope Meg will remember that children should be children as long as they can."

"I don't call myself a child, and I'm not in my teens yet," observed Amy. "What do you say, Beth?"

"I was thinking about our Pilgrim's Progress," answered Beth. How we got out of the Slough and through the Wicket Gate by resolving to be good, and up the steep hill by trying; and that maybe the house over there is going to be our Palace Beautiful."

## CHAPTER SIX

# BETH FINDS THE PALACE BEAUTIFUL

The Big House did prove a Palace Beautiful, though it took some time for all to get in. Old Mr. Laurence called, said something funny or kind to each one of the girls, and talked over old times with their mother; nobody felt afraid of him, except timid Beth. The fact that they were poor and Laurie rich made them shy of accepting favours which they could not return. But after a while they found that he considered them the benefactors, and could not do enough to show how grateful he was for Mrs. March's motherly welcome, their cheerful society, and the comfort he took in that humble home of theirs; so they soon forgot their pride, and interchanged kindnesses without stopping to think which was the greater.

All sorts of pleasant things happened about that time. Everybody liked Laurie, and he informed his tutor that "the Marches were reguarly splendid girls." They took the solitary boy into their midst, and he found something very charming in the innocent companionship of these simple-hearted girls. Never having known mother or sisters, he was quick to feel the influences they brought about him; and their busy, lively ways made him ashamed of the indolent life he led. He was tired of books, and found people so interesting now that Mr. Brooke was obliged to make very unsatisfactory reports; for Laurie was always playing truant, and running over to the Marches.

"Never mind, let him take a holiday, and make it up afterwards," said the old gentleman. "The good lady next door says he is studying too hard, and needs young society. I suspect she is right."

What good times they had! Such plays and tableaux; such sleigh-rides and skating frolics; such pleasant evenings in the old parlour, and now and then such gay little parties at the great house.

But Beth, though yearning for the grand piano, could not pluck up courage to go to the "mansion of bliss." She went once with Jo, but the old gentleman, not being aware of her infirmity, stared at her so hard from under his heavy brows, and said "hey!" so loud, that he frightened her so much her "feet chattered on the floor," she told her mother; and she ran away. No persuasions could overcome her fear, till the fact coming to Mr. Laurence's ear, he set about mending matters. During one of the brief calls he made, he artfully led the conversation to music, and talked about great singers whom he had heard, and told such charming anecdotes, that Beth found it impossible to stay in her distant corner, but crept nearer and nearer, as if fascinated. At the back of his chair she stopped, and stood listening with her great eyes wide open, and her cheeks red with excitement. Mr. Laurence talked on about Laurie's lessons and teachers; and presently he said to Mrs. March, —

"The boy neglects his music now, and I'm glad of it, for he was getting too fond of it. But the piano suffers for want of use; wouldn't some of your girls like to run over and practise on it now and then, just to keep it in tune?"

Beth took a step forward, and pressed her hands tightly together, to keep from clapping them, for this was an irresistible temptation; and the thought of practising on that splendid instrument quite took her breath away. Before Mrs. March could reply, Mr. Laurence went on: "They needn't see or speak to anyone, but run in at any time, for I'm shut up in my study at the other end of the house."

Here he rose, as if going, and Beth made up her mind to speak, for that arrangement left nothing to be desired. "Please tell the young ladies what I say, and if they don't care to come, why, never mind." Here a little hand slipped into his, and Beth looked up at him with a face full of gratitude, as she said, in her earnest, timid way, "Oh, sir! they do care, very, very much!"

"Are you the musical girl?" he asked without any startling "hey!" as he looked down at her very kindly.

"I'm Beth; I love it dearly, and I'll come if you are quite sure nobody will hear me — and be disturbed," she added, fearing to be rude.

"Not a soul, my dear. The house is empty half the day, so come and drum away as much as you like, and I shall be obliged to you."

"How kind you are, sir!"

Beth blushed like a rose under the friendly look he wore, but she was not frightened now, and gave the big hand a grateful squeeze because she had no words to thank him for the previous gift he had given her. The old gentleman softly stroked the hair off her forehead, and, stooping down, he kissed her, saying, in a tone few people ever heard, "I had a little girl once with eyes like these. God bless you, my dear! Good day, madam"; and away he went, in a great hurry.

Beth had a rapture with her mother, and then rushed up to impart the glorious news to her family of invalids. How blithely she sang that evening, and how they all laughed at her, because she woke Amy in the night by playing the piano on her face in her sleep. Quite by accident, of course, some pretty easy music lay on the piano; and, with trembling fingers and frequent stops to listen and look about, Beth at last touched the great instrument, and straightway forgot her fear, herself, and everything else but the delight which the music gave her.

She stayed till Hannah came to take her home to dinner; but she had no appetite, and could only sit and smile upon everyone in a great state of beatitude.

After that, the little brown hood slipped through the hedge nearly every day, and the great drawing-room was haunted by a tuneful spirit that came and went unseen. She never knew that Mr. Laurence often opened his study door to hear the old-fashioned airs he liked; she never saw Laurie mount guard in the hall, to warn the servants away; she never suspected that the exercise-books and new songs which she found in the rack were put there for her special benefit; and when he talked to her about music at home, she only thought how kind he was to tell things that helped her so much.

"Mother, I'm going to work Mr. Laurence a pair of slippers. He is so kind to me, I must thank him, and I don't know any other way. Can I do it?" asked Bethy a few weeks after that eventful call of his.

"Yes, dear; it will please him very much, and be a nice way of thanking him. The girls will help you about them, and I will pay for the making up," replied Mrs. March, who took peculiar pleasure in granting Beth's requests, because she so seldom asked anything for herself.

After many serious discussions with Meg and Jo, the pattern was chosen, the materials bought, and the slippers begun. A cluster of grave yet cheerful pansies, on a deeper purple ground, was pronounced very appropriate, and Beth worked away early and late, with occasional lifts over hard parts. She was a nimble little needlewoman, and they were finished before anyone got tired of them. Then she wrote a very short, simple note, and, with Laurie's help, got them smuggled on to the study table one morning before the old gentleman was up.

When this excitement was over, Beth waited to see what would happen. All that day passed, and a part of the next, before any acknowledgement arrived, and she was beginning to fear she had offended her crotchety friend. On the afternoon of the second day she went out to do an errand, and give poor Joanna, the invalid doll, her daily exercise. As she came up the street on her return, she saw four heads popping in and out of the parlour windows and the moment they saw her several hands were waved, and several joyful voices screamed, "Here's a letter from the old gentleman; come quick and read it!"

Beth hurried in a twitter of suspense; at the door her sisters seized her and bore her to the parlour in a triumphal procession, all pointing, and all saying at once, "Look there! look there!" Beth did look, and turned pale with delight and surprise; for there stood a little cabinet piano, with a letter lying on the glossy lid, directed, like a signboard, to "Miss Elizabeth March."

"For me?" gasped Beth, holding on to Jo.

"Yes; all for you, my precious! Isn't it splendid of him? Here's the key in the letter; we didn't open it, but we are dying to know what he says," cried Jo, offering the note.

"You read it; I can't, I feel so queer. Oh, it is too lovely!" and Beth hid her face in Jo's apron.

Jo opened the paper, and began to laugh, for the first words she saw were: —

" 'Miss March:

" 'Dear Madam —

" 'I have had many pairs of slippers in my life but I never had any that suited me so well as yours,' " continued Jo.

" 'Heart's-ease is my favourite flower, and these will always remind me of the gentle giver. I like to pay my debts, so I know you will allow "the old gentleman" to send you something which once belonged to the little grand-daughter he lost. With hearty thanks and best wishes, I remain,

" *'Your grateful friend and humble servant,*
" *'James Laurence.'* "

"There, Beth, that's an honour to be proud of, I'm sure! Laurie told me how fond Mr. Laurence used to be of the child who died, and how he kept all her things carefully. Just think; he's given you her piano! That comes of having big blue eyes and loving music," said Jo, trying to soothe Beth, who trembled, and looked more excited than she had ever been before.

"Try it, honey, let's hear the sound of the baby pianny," said Hannah, who always took a share in the family joys and sorrows.

So Beth tried it, and everyone pronounced it the most remarkable piano ever heard. It had evidently been newly tuned, and put in apple-pie order.

"You'll have to go and thank him," said Jo, by way of a joke, for the idea of the child's really going never entered her hear.

"Yes, I mean to; I guess I'll go now, before I get frightened thinking about it"; and, to the utter amazement of the assembled family, Beth walked down the garden, through the hedge, and in at the Laurence's door.

"Well, I wish I may die if it ain't the queerest thing I ever see! The pianny has turned her head; she'd never have gone in her right mind," cried Hannah, staring after her, while the girls were rendered speechless by the miracle.

54

They would have been still more amazed if they had seen what Beth did afterward. She went and knocked at the study door; and when a gruff voice called out, "Come in!" she did go in, right up to Mr. Laurence, and held out her hand, saying, with only a small quaver in her voice, "I came to thank you, sir, for —" but she didn't finish, for he looked so friendly that she forgot her speech; and only remembering that he had lost the little girl he loved, she put both arms round his neck and kissed him.

If the roof of the house had suddenly flown off, the old gentleman wouldn't have been more astonished; but he liked it — oh, dear, yes! he liked it amazingly; and was so touched and pleased by that confiding little kiss that all his crustiness vanished; and he just set her on his knee, and laid his wrinkled cheek against her rosy one, feeling as if he had got his own little grand-daughter back again. Beth ceased to fear him from that moment, and sat there talking to him as cosily as if she had known him all her life; for love casts out fear. When she went home, he walked with her to her own gate, shook hands cordially, and touched his hat as he marched back again looking very stately and erect.

When the girls saw the performance, Jo began to dance a jig; Amy nearly fell out of the window in her surprise, and Meg exclaimed, with uplifted hands, "Well, I do believe the world is coming to an end!"

## CHAPTER SEVEN
## AMY'S VALLEY OF HUMILIATION

"That boy is a perfect Cyclops, isn't he?" said Amy, one day, as Laurie clattered by on horseback.

"Oh, my goodness! That little goose means a centaur, and she called him a Cyclops!" exclaimed Jo, with a burst of laughter.

"You needn't be so rude; it's only a 'lapse of lingy', as Mr. Davis says," retorted Amy, finishing Jo with her Latin. "I just wish I had a little of the money Laurie spends on that horse."

"Why?" asked Meg.

"I need it so much; I'm dreadfully in debt, and it won't be my turn to have the rag-money for a month."

"In debt, Amy; what do you mean?"

"Why, I owe at least a dozen pickled limes."

"Tell me about it. Are limes the fashion now? It used to be pricking bits of rubber to make balls"; and Meg tried to keep her countenance, Amy looked so grave and important.

"Why, you see, the girls are always buying them, and unless you want to be thought mean, you must do it, too. If one girl likes another, she gives her a lime; if she's mad with her, she eats one before her face. They treat by turns; and I've had ever so many, but haven't returned them."

"How much will restore your credit?" asked Meg, taking out her purse.

"A quarter would more than do it."

"Here's the money; make it last as long as you can, for it isn't very plentiful, you know."

"Oh, thank you! I'll have a grand feast, for I haven't tasted a lime this week. I felt delicate about taking any, as I couldn't return them."

Next day, Amy was rather late at school; but could not resist the temptation of displaying a moist brown paper parcel, before she consigned it to the inmost recesses of her desk. During the next few minutes the rumour that Amy March had got twenty-four delicious limes (she ate one on the way), and was going to treat, circulated through her "set," and the attentions of her friends became quite overwhelming. Kate Brown invited her to her next party on the spot; Mary Kingsley insisted on lending her her watch till recess, and Jenny Snow, a satirical young lady who had basely twitted Amy upon her limeless state, promptly buried the hatchet, and offered to furnish answers to certain appalling sums. But Amy had not forgotten Miss Snow's cutting remarks about "Some persons whose noses were not too flat to smell other people's limes," and she instantly crushed "That Snow girl's" hopes by the withering telegram, "You needn't be so polite all of a sudden, for you won't get any."

A distinguished personage happened to visit the school that morning, and Amy's beautifully drawn maps received praise, which honour to her foe rankled in the soul of Miss Snow, and caused Miss March to assume the airs of a studious young peacock. But alas! pride goes before a fall, and the revengeful Snow turned the tables with disastrous success. No sooner had the guest bowed himself out, than Jenny, under pretence of asking an important question, informed Mr. Davis, the teacher, that Amy March had pickled limes in her desk.

Now, Mr. Davis had declared limes a contraband item, and vowed to ferule the first person who was found breaking the law. Mr. Davis had evidently taken his coffee too strong that morning; there was an east wind, which always affected his neuralgia, and his pupils had not done him the credit which he felt he deserved. The word "limes" was like fire to powder; his yellow face flushed, and he rapped on his desk with an energy which made Jenny skip to her seat with unusual rapidity.

"Young ladies, attention, if you please!"

At the stern order the buzz ceased, and fifty pairs of blue, black, grey, and brown eyes were obediently fixed upon his awful countenance.

57

"Miss March, come to the desk."

Amy rose to comply, with outward composure; but a secret fear oppressed her, for the limes weighed upon her conscience.

"Bring with you the limes you have in your desk," was the unexpected command.

"Don't take all," whispered her neighbour, a young lad of great presence of mind.

Amy hastily shook out half a dozen, and laid the rest down before Mr. Davis.

"Is that all?"

"Not quite," stammered Amy.

"Bring the rest immediately."

With a despairing glance at her set she obeyed.

"You are sure there are no more?"

"I never, lie, sir."

"So I see. Now take these disgusting things, two by two, and throw them out of the window."

Scarlet with shame and anger, Amy went to and fro twelve mortal times and as each doomed couple — looking, oh, so plump and juicy! fell from her reluctant hands, a shout from the street completed the anguish of the girls, for it told them that their feast was being exulted over by the little Irish children who were their sworn foes. This was too much; all flashed indignant glances at the inexorable Davis, and one passionate lime-lover burst into tears.

As Amy returned from her last trip, Mr. Davis gave a portentous "hem" and said, "Young ladies, you remember what I said to you a week ago. I never allow my rules to be infringed, and I *never* break my word. Miss March, hold out your hand."

Amy started, and put both hands behind her, turning on him an imploring look. She was rather a favourite with "old Davis," and it's my private belief that he *would* have broken his word if the indignation of one irrepressible young lady had not found vent in a hiss.

"Your hand, Miss March!" was the only answer her mute appeal received; and, too proud to cry or beseech, Amy set her teeth, threw back her head defiantly, and bore without flinching several tingling blows on her little palm. They were neither many nor heavy, but that made no difference to her. For the first time in her life she had been struck; and the disgrace, in her eyes was as deep as if he had knocked her down.

"You will now stand on the platform till recess," said Mr. Davis.

That was dreadful. It would have been bad enough to go to her seat and see the pitying faces of her friends; but to face the whole school with that shame fresh upon her seemed impossible and for a second she felt as if she could only drop down and break her heart with crying. A bitter sense of wrong and the thought of Jenny Snow, helped her to bear it; and, taking the ignominious place, she fixed her eyes on the stove-funnel and stood there so motionless and white, that the girls found it very hard to study with that pathetic little figure before them.

During the fifteen minutes that followed, the proud and sensitive little girl suffered a shame and pain which she never forgot. The smart of her hand, and the ache of her heart were forgotten in the sting of the thought, "I shall have to tell at home, and they will be so disappointed in me."

The fifteen minutes seemed an hour; but they came to an end at last, and the word "recess !" had never seemed so welcome to her before.

"You can go, Miss March," said Mr. Davis, looking, as he felt, uncomfortable.

He did not soon forget the reproachful look Amy gave him, as she went, without a word to anyone, straight into the anteroom, snatched her things, and left the place "for ever," as she passionately declared to herself. She was in a sad state when she got home; and when the older girls arrived, some time later, an indignation meeting was held at once. Mrs. March did not say much, but looked disturbed, and comforted her afflicted little daughter in her tenderest manner. Meg bathed the insulted hand with glycerine and tears; Beth felt that even her beloved kittens would fail as a balm for griefs like this; and Jo wrathfully proposed that Mr. Davis be arrested without delay, while Hannah shook her fist at the "villain," and pounded potatoes for dinner as if she had him under her pestle.

No notice was taken of Amy's flight, except by her mates; but the sharp-eyed demoiselles discovered that Mr. Davis was quite benignant in the afternoon — also unusually nervous. Just before school closed, Jo appeared, wearing a grim expression as she stalked up to the desk and delivered a letter from her mother; then collected Amy's property and departed, carefully scraping the mud from her boots on the door-mat.

"Yes, you can have a vacation from school but I want you to study a little every day with Beth," said Mrs. March that evening. "I don't approve of corporal punishment, especially for girls. I dislike Mr. Davis's manner of teaching, and don't think the girls you associate with are doing you any good, so I shall ask your father's advice before I send you anywhere else."

"That's good! I wish all the girls would leave and spoil his old school. It's perfectly maddening to think of those lovely limes," sighed Amy, with the air of a martyr.

"I am not sorry you lost them, for you broke the rules, and deserved some punishment for disobedience," was the severe reply, which rather disappointed the young lady, who expected nothing but sympathy.

"Do you mean you are glad I was disgraced before the whole school?" cried Amy.

"I should not have chosen that way of mending the fault," replied her mother; "but I'm not sure that it won't do you more good than a milder method. You are getting to be rather conceited, my dear, and it is quite time you set about correcting it. You have a good many little gifts and virtues, but there is no need of parading them, for conceit spoils the finest genius. There is not much danger that real talent or goodness will be overlooked long; even if it is, the consciousness of possessing and using it well should satisfy one, and the great charm of all power is modesty."

"So it is!" cried Laurie, who was playing chess in a corner with Jo. "I knew a girl, once, who had a really remarkable talent for music, and she didn't know it; never guessed what sweet little things she composed when she was alone, and wouldn't have believed it if any one had told her."

"I wish I'd known that nice girl; maybe she would have helped me, I'm so stupid," said Beth, who stood beside him, listening eagerly.

"You do know her, and she helps you better than anyone else could," answered Laurie, looking at her with such mischievous meaning in his merry black eyes, that Beth suddenly turned very red, and hid her face in the sofa-cushion, quite overcome by such an unexpected discovery.

Jo let Laurie win the game, to pay for that praise of her Beth, who could not be prevailed upon to play for them after her compliment. So Laurie did his best, and sung delightfully, being in a particularly lively humor, for to the Marches he seldom showed the moody side of his character. When he was gone, Amy, who had been pensive all the evening, said suddenly, as if busy over some new idea, —

"Is Laurie an accomplished boy?"

"Yes; he has had an excellent education, and has much talent; he will make a fine man, if not spoilt by petting," replied her mother.

"And he isn't conceited, is he?" asked Amy.

"Not in the least; that is why he is so charming, and we all like him so much."

"I see; it's nice to have accomplishments, and be elegant; but not to show off, or get perked up," said Amy thoughtfully.

"These things are always seen and felt in a person's manner and conversation, if modestly used; but it is not necessary to display them," said Mrs. March.

"Any more than it's proper to wear all your bonnets and gowns and ribbons at once, that folks may know you've got them," added Jo; and the lecture ended in a laugh.


CHAPTER EIGHT

## JO MEETS APOLLYON

"Girls, where are you going?" asked Amy, coming into their room one Saturday afternoon, and finding them getting ready to go out, with an air of secrecy which excited her curiosity.

"Never mind; little girls shouldn't ask questions," returned Jo sharply.

"I know! I know! You're going to the theatre to see the *Seven Castles!*" she cried; adding resolutely, "and *I shall* go, for mother said I might see it; and I've got my rag-money."

"Just listen to me a minute, and be a good child," said Meg soothingly. "Next week you can go with Beth and Hannah, and have a nice time."

"I don't like that half so well as going with you and Laurie. Please let me. Do, Meg! I'll be ever so good," pleaded Amy.

"Suppose we take her? I don't believe mother would mind," began Meg.

"If she goes, I shan't; and if I don't Laurie won't like it; and it will be very rude, after he invited only us, to go and drag in Amy, I should think she'd hate to poke herself where she isn't wanted," said Jo crossly.

Her tone and manner angered Amy who began to put her boots on, saying, "I shall go; Meg says I may; and if I pay for myself, Laurie hasn't anything to do with it."

"You shan't stir a step; so you may just stay where you are," scolded Jo.

Siting on the floor, with one boot on, Amy began to cry, and Meg to reason with her, when Laurie called from below, and the two girls hurried down, leaving their sister wailing.

They had a charming time, for *The Seven Castles of the Diamond Lake* was as wonderful as heart could wish. But Jo's pleasure had a drop of biterness in it; the fairy queen's yellow curls reminded her of Amy.

When they got home, they found Amy reading in the parlour. She assumed an injured air as they came in; never lifted her eyes from her book, or asked a single question. On going up to put away her best hat, Jo's first look was towards the bureau; for, in their last quarrel, Amy had soothed her feelings by turning Jo's top drawer upside down, on the floor. Everything was in its place, however, and after a hasty glance into her various closets, bags, and boxes, Jo decided that Amy had forgotten and forgiven her wrongdoings.

There Jo was mistaken; for next day she made a discovery which produced a tempest. Meg, Beth and Amy were sitting together, late in the afternoon, when Jo burst into the room and demanded breathlessly, "Has anyone taken my story?"

Meg and Beth said, "No," at once, and looked surprised; Amy poked the fire, and said nothing.

"Amy, you've got it!"

"No, I haven't."

"That's a fib!" cried Jo, taking her by the shoulders.

"It isn't. I haven't got it; don't know where it is now, and don't care."

"You know something about it, and you'd better tell at once, or I'll make you"; and Jo gave her a slight shake.

"Scold as much as you like, you'll never get your silly old story again," cried Amy.

"Why not?"

"I burnt it up."

"What! My little book I was so fond of, and worked over, and meant to finish before father got home? Have you really burnt it?" said Jo, turning very pale.

"Yes, I did!"

Amy got no further, for Jo's hot temper mastered her, and she shook Amy till her teeth chattered in her head; crying, in a passion of grief and anger, — "You wicked, wicked, girl! I never can write it again, and I'll never forgive you as long as I live."

Meg flew to rescue Amy, and Beth to pacify Jo, but Jo was quite beside herself; and, with a parting box on her sister's ear, she rushed out of the room up to the old sofa in the garret, and finished her fight alone.

The storm cleared up below, for Mrs. March came home, and, having heard the story, soon brought Amy to a sense of the wrong she had done her sister. Jo's book was the pride of her heart, and was regarded by her family as a literary sprout of great promise. It was only half a dozen little fairy tales, but Jo had worked over them patiently, putting her whole heart into her work, hoping to make something good enough to print. She had just copied them with great care, and had destroyed the old manuscript, so that Amy's bonfire had consumed the loving work of several years. It seemed a small loss to others, but to Jo it was a dreadful calamity. Beth mourned as for a departed kitten, and Meg refused to defend her pet; Mrs. March looked grieved, and Amy felt that no one would love her till she had asked pardon for the act which she now regretted.

When the tea bell rang, Jo appeared, looking so grim and unapproachable that it took all Amy's courage to say meekly, "Please forgive me, Jo; I'm very, very sorry."

"I shall never forgive you," was Jo's stern answer; and, from that moment, she ignored Amy entirely.

No one spoke of the great trouble, — not even Mrs. March, for all had learned by experience that when Jo was in that mood words were wasted. It was not a happy evening; for though they sewed as usual, while their mother read aloud, something was wanting, and the sweet home-peace was disturbed. They felt this most when singing-time came, and Amy broke down. So Meg and her mother sang alone.

As Jo received her good-night kiss, Mrs. March whispered, gently, — "My dear, don't let the sun go down upon your anger."

Jo wanted to lay her head down on that motherly bosom and cry her grief and anger all away; but she felt so deeply injured that she really *couldn't* quite forget yet. So she winked hard, shook her head and said, gruffly, because Amy was listening, — "It was an abominable thing, and she didn't deserve to be forgiven."

With that she marched off to bed, and there was no merry gossip that night.

Amy was much offended that her overtures of peace had been repulsed, and began to plume herself on her superior virtue. Jo still looked like a thunder-cloud, and nothing went well that day.

"Everybody is so hateful, I'll ask Laurie to go skating," said Jo to herself, and off she went.

Amy heard the clash of skates, and looked out with an impatient exclamation, — "There! she promised I should go next time. But it is no use to ask such a cross-patch to take me."

"Don't say that; you *were* very naughty, and it is hard to forgive the loss of her precious little book; but I think she might do it now, and I guess she will, if you try her at the right minute," said Meg. "Go after them; don't say anything till Jo has got good natured with Laurie, then just kiss her, or do some kind thing, and I'm sure she'll be friends again."

"I'll try," said Amy; and she ran after the friends, who were just disappearing over the hill.

It was not far to the river, but both were ready before Amy reached them. Jo saw her coming, and turned her back; Laurie did not see, for he was skating along the shore, sounding the ice, for a warm spell had preceded the cold snap.

"I'll go to the first bend, and see if it's all right, before we begin to race," Amy heard him say, as he shot away, looking like a young Russian in his fur-trimmed coat and cap.

Jo heard Amy panting after her run, stamping her feet, and blowing her fingers, as she tried to put her skates on; but Jo never turned, and went slowly zigzagging down the river, taking a bitter, unhappy sort of satisfaction in her sister's troubles. As Laurie turned the bend, he shouted back, — "Keep near the shore; it isn't safe in the middle."

Jo heard, but Amy was just struggling to her feet, and did not catch a word. Jo glanced over her shoulder, and the little demon she was harbouring said in her ear, — "No matter whether she heard or not; let her take care of herself."

Laurie had vanished round the bend; Jo was just at the turn, and Amy, far behind, striking out toward the smoother ice in the middle of the river. For a moment Jo stood still, with a strange feeling at her heart; then she resolved to go on, but something held and turned her round, just in time to see Amy throw up her hands and go down, with the sudden crash of rotten ice, and the splash of water, and a cry that made Jo's heart stand still with fear. She tried to call Laurie, but her voice was gone; she tried to rush forward, but her feet seemed to have no strength in them; and, for a second, she could only stand motionless, staring, with a terror-stricken face, at the little blue hood above the black water. Something rushed swiftly by her, and Laurie's voice called out, —

"Bring a rail; quick, quick!" How she did it she never knew, but the next few minutes she worked as if possessed, blindly obeying Laurie, who, lying flat, held Amy up by his arms, till Jo dragged a rail from the fence, and together they got the child out, more frightened than hurt.

"Now then, we must walk her home as fast as we can; pile our things on her, while I get off these confounded skates," cried Laurie, wrapping his coat round Amy, and tugging away at the straps.

Shivering, dripping, and crying, they got Amy home; and, after an exciting time of it, she fell asleep, rolled in blankets, before a hot fire. During the bustle Jo had scarcely spoken, but flown about, looking pale and wild, with her things half off, her dress torn, and her hands cut and bruised. When Amy was asleep, the house quiet, and Mrs. March sitting by the bed, she called Jo to her and began to bind up the hurt hands.

"Are you sure she is safe?" whispered Jo, looking remorsefully at the golden head.

"Quite safe, dear; she is not hurt, and won't even take cold, I think; you were so sensible in covering and getting her home quickly."

"Laurie did it all; I only let her go. Mother, if she *should* die, it would be my fault"; and Jo dropped down beside the bed, in a passion of penitent tears, telling all that had happened.

"It's my dreadful temper! I try to cure it; I think I have, and then it breaks out worse than ever. Oh, mother! what shall I do? It seems as if I could do anything when I'm in a passion; I get so savage, I could hurt anyone. I'm afraid I *shall* do something dreadful some day, and spoil my life, and make everybody hate me. Oh, mother, help me."

"I will, my child. Don't cry so bitterly, but remember this day, and resolve that you will never know another like it. Jo, dear, we all have our temptations, and it often takes us all our lives to conquer them. You think your temper is the worst in the world, but mine used to be just like it."

"Yours, mother? Why, you are never angry!"

"I've been trying to cure it for forty years, and have only succeeded in controlling it. I am angry nearly every day of my life, Jo; but I have learned not to show it."

The patience and the humility of the face she loved so well was a beter lesson to Jo than the wisest lecture. She felt comforted at once by the sympathy and confidence given her; the knowledge that her mother had a fault like hers, and tried to mend it, made her own easier to bear.

"Mother, are you angry when you fold your lips tight together, and go out of the room sometimes, when Aunt March scolds, or people worry you?" asked Jo.

"Yes; I've learned to check the hasty words that rise to my lips, and when I feel that they mean to break out again against my will, I just go away a minute, and give myself a little shake, for being so weak and wicked," answered Mrs. March.

"How did you learn to keep still? Tell me how you do it, Marmee, dear."

"My good mother used to help me —"

"As you do us," interrupted Jo.

"But I lost her when I was a little older than you are, and for years had to struggle on alone. I had a hard time, Jo, and shed many bitter tears over my failures. Then your father came, and I was so happy that I found it easy to be good. But when I had four little daughters round me, and we were poor, the old trouble began again."

"Poor mother! what helped you then?"

"Your father, Jo. He never loses patience, but always hopes, and works and waits so cheerfully that one is ashamed to do otherwise before him. He showed me that I must try to practise all the virtues I would have my little girls possess, for I was their example. A startled or surprised look from one of you, when I spoke sharply, rebuked me more than any words could have done; and the love of my children was the sweetest reward I could receive."

"Oh, mother! if I'm ever half as good as you, I shall be satisfied," cried Jo, much troubled.

"I hope you will be a great deal better, dear; but you must keep watch over your 'bosom enemy'."

Amy stirred, and sighed in her sleep; and, as if eager to begin at once to mend her fault, Jo looked up with an expression on her face which it had never worn before.

"I let the sun go down on my anger; I wouldn't forgive her, and today, if it hadn't been for Laurie, it might have been too late! How could I have been so wicked?" said Jo half aloud, as she leaned over her sister, softly stroking the wet hair scattered over the pillow.

As if she heard, Amy opened her eyes, and held out her arms, with a smile that went straight to Jo's heart. Neither said a word, but they hugged one another close, and everything was forgotten and forgiven in one hearty kiss.

CHAPTER NINE

## MEG GOES TO VANITY FAIR

"I do think it was the most fortunate thing in the world that those children should have the measles just now," said Meg, one April day, as she stood packing the "go-abroady" trunk.

"And so nice of Annie Moffat not to forget her promise. A whole fortnight of fun will be splendid," replied Jo, looking like a windmill, as she folded skirts with her long arms.

"And such lovely weather; I'm so glad of that," added Beth, tidily sorting neck and hair ribbons.

"I wish I was going to wear all these nice things," said Amy.

"I wish you were all going; but, as you can't, I shall keep my adventures to tell you when I come back. It's the least I can do, when you have been so kind, lending me things, and helping me get ready," said Meg, glancing round the room at the simple outfit which seemed nearly perfect in their eyes.

"What did mother give you out of the treasure-box?" asked Amy.

"A pair of silk stockings, that pretty carved fan, and a lovely blue sash. I wanted the violet silk; but there isn't time to make it over, so I must be contented with my old tarlatan."

"It will look nicely over my new muslin skirt, and the sash will set it off beautifully. I wish I hadn't smashed my coral bracelet, for you might have had it," said Jo, who loved to give and lend.

"There is a lovely old-fashioned pearl set in the treasure-box; but mother said real flowers were the prettiest ornament for a young girl, and Laurie promised to send me all I want," replied Meg. "Now, let me see; there's my new grey walking suit — just curl up the feather in my hat, Beth; — then my poplin, for Sunday, and the small party — it looks heavy for spring, doesn't it? The violet silk would be so nice; oh, dear!"

"Never mind; you've got the tarlatan for the big party, and you always look like an angel in white," said Amy.

"It isn't low-necked, and it doesn't sweep enough, but it will have to do. My silk stockings and two pairs of spandy gloves are my comfort. You are a dear to lend me yours, Jo. I feel so elegant, with two new pairs, and the old ones cleaned up for common"; and Meg took a refreshing peep at her glove-box. "I wonder if I shall *ever* be happy enough to have real lace on my clothes, and bows on my caps?"

"You said the other day that you'd be perfectly happy if you could only go to Annie Moffat's," observed Beth in her quiet way.

"So I did! Well, I *am* happy, and I *won't* fret; but it does seem as if the more one gets the more one wants, doesn't it? There, now, the trays are ready, and everything in but my balldress, which I shall leave for mother," said Meg, cheering up, as she glanced from the half-filled trunk to the many-times pressed, and mended white tarlatan which she called her "balldress," with an important air.

The Moffats *were* very fashionable, and simple Meg was rather daunted, at first, by the splendour of the house and the elegance of its occupants. It was agreeable to fare sumptuously, drive in a fine carriage, wear her best frock every day, and do nothing but enjoy herself. Soon she began to imitate the manners and conversation of those about her; to put on little airs and graces, and talk about the fashions. The more she saw of Annie Moffat's pretty things, the more she envied them.

When the evening for the "small party" came, she found that the poplin wouldn't do at all; so out came the tarlatan, looking older, limper, and shabbier than ever, beside Sallie's crisp new one. No one said a word about it, but Sallie offered to do her hair, and Annie to tie her sash, and Belle, the engaged sister, praised her white arms; but, in their kindness, Meg saw only pity for her poverty, and her heart felt very heavy. The hard bitter feeling was getting pretty bad, when the maid brought in a box of flowers. Before she could speak, Annie had the cover off, and all were exclaiming at the lovely roses, heath, and ferns within.

"It's for Belle, of course; George always sends her some but these are altogether ravishing," cried Annie, with a great sniff.

"They are for Miss March, the man said. And here's a note," put in the maid, holding it to Meg.

"What fun! Who are they from? Didn't know you had a lover," cried the girls.

"The note is from mother, and the flowers from Laurie," said Meg simply.

"Oh, indeed!" said Annie, with a funny look, as Meg slipped the note into her pocket, as a sort of talisman against envy, vanity, and false pride; for the few loving words had done her good, and the flowers cheered her up by their beauty.

Feeling almost happy again, she laid by a few ferns and roses for herself, and made up the rest in dainty bouquets for the breasts, hair, or skirts of her friends, offering them so pretty that Clara, the elder sister, told her she was "the sweetest little thing she ever saw." Somehow the kind act finished her despondency; and, when all the rest went to show themselves to Mrs. Moffat, she saw a happy, bright-eyed face in the mirror, as she laid her ferns against her rippling hair, and fastened the roses in the dress that didn't strike her as so *very* shabby now.

She enjoyed herself very much that evening, for she danced to her heart's content; everyone was very kind, and she had three compliments. Annie made her sing, and some-one said she had a remarkably fine voice; Major Lincoln asked who "the fresh little girl, with the beautiful eyes was"; and Mr. Moffat insisted on dancing with her because she "didn't dawdle, but had some spring in her." So altogether, she had a very nice time, till she overheard a bit of conversation. She was sitting just inside the conservatory, waiting for her partner to bring her an ice, when she heard a voice ask, — "How old is she?"

"Sixteen or seventeen, I should say," replied another voice.

"It would be a grand thing for one of those girls, wouldn't it?"

"Mrs. M. has laid her plans, I dare say, and will play her cards well. The girl evidently doesn't think of it yet," said Mrs. Moffat.

"She told that fib about her mamma, as if she did know, and coloured up when the flowers came, quite prettily. Poor thing! she'd be so nice if she was only got up in style. Do you think she'd be offended if we offered to lend her a dress for Thursday?" asked another voice.

"She's proud, but I don't believe she'd mind, for that dowdy tarlatan is all she has got. She may tear it tonight, and that will be a good excuse for offering a decent one."

"We'll see; I shall ask that Laurence as a compliment to her, and we'll have fun about it afterward."

Here Meg's partner appeared to find her looking flushed and agitated. She was proud, and her pride was useful just then, for it helped her hide her anger and disgust at what she had just heard; for, innocent as she was, she could not help understanding the gossip of her friends. She did her best to seem gay; and succeeded so well that no one dreamed what an effort she was making.

Poor Meg had a restless night, and got up heavy-eyed. Something in the manner of her friends struck Meg at once; they treated her with more respect, she thought, and looked at her with eyes that plainly betrayed curiosity. All this surprised and flattered her, though she did not understand it till Miss Belle said, with a sentimental air, —

"Daisy, dear, I've sent an invitation to your friend, Mr. Laurence, for Thursday."

Meg coloured, but a mischievous fancy to tease the girls made her reply demurely, — "You are very kind, but I'm afraid he won't come."

"Why not, *chérie?*" asked Miss Belle.

"He's too old."

"My child, what do you mean? What is his age, I beg to know?" cried Miss Clara.

"Nearly seventy, I believe," answered Meg.

"You sly creature! Of course, we meant he young man," exclaimed Miss Belle, laughing.

"There isn't any; Laurie is only a little boy."

"About your age?" Nan said.

"Nearer my sister Jo's; *I* am seventeen in August," returned Meg, tossing her head.

"It's very nice of him to send you flowers, isn't it?" said Annie.

"Yes; he often does, to all of us; for their house is full, and we are so fond of them. My mother and old Mr. Laurence are friends, so it's quite natural we children should play together."

"It's evident Daisy isn't out yet," said Miss Clara to Belle, with a nod.

"I am going out to get some little matters for my girls; can I do anything for you, young ladies?" asked Mrs. Moffat, lumbering in like an elephant, in silk and lace.

"No thank you, ma'am," replied Sallie; "I've got my new pink silk for Thursday, and don't want a thing."

"Nor I —" began Meg, but stopped, because it occurred to her that she *did* want several things, and could not have them.

"What shall you wear?" asked Sallie.

"My old white one again, if I can mend it fit to be seen; it got sadly torn last night," said Meg.

"Why don't you send home for another?" asked Sallie, who was not an observing young lady. "I haven't got any other." It cost Meg an effort to say that, but Sallie did not see it, and exclaimed in amiable surprise, — "Only that? how funny —" She did not finish her speech, for Belle shook her head at her, and broke in, saying kindly, — "Not at all; where is the use of having a lot of dresses when she isn't out? I've got a sweet blue silk laid away which I've outgrown, and you shall wear it to please me."

"You are very kind, but I don't mind my old dress if you don't; it does well enough for a little girl like me," said Meg.

"Now do let me please myself by dressing you up in style. You'd be a regular little beauty with a touch here and there. I shan't let anyone see you till you are done, and then we'll burst upon them like Cinderella and her godmother going to the ball," said Belle, in her persuasive tone.

Meg couldn't refuse the offer so kindly made, for a desire to see if she would be "a litle beauty" after touching up caused her to accept and forget all her former uncomfortable feelings towards the Moffats.

On the Thursday evening Belle shut herself up with her maid, and, between them, they turned Meg into a fine lady. They crimpled and curled her hair, they polished her neck and arms with some fragrant powder, touched her lips with coralline salve, to make them redder, and Hortense would have added "a *soupçon* of rouge," if Meg had not rebelled. They laced her into a sky-blue dress, which was so tight she could hardly breathe, and so low in the neck that modest Meg blushed at herself in the mirror. A set of silver filigree was added, bracelets, necklace, brooch, and even ear-rings. A cluster of tea rosebuds at the bosom, and a *ruche*, reconciled Meg to the display of her pretty white shoulders, and a pair of high-heeled blue silk boots satisfied the last wish of her heart. A lace handkerchief, a plumy fan, and a bouquet in a silver holder finished her off.

"*Mademoiselle est charmante, très jolie*, is she not?" cried Hortense.

"Come and show youself," said Miss Belle, leading the way to the room where the others were waiting.

As Meg went rustling after, with her long skirts trailing, her ear-rings tinkled, her curls waving, and her heart beating, she felt as if her "fun" had really begun at last, for the mirror had plainly told her that she *was* "a little beauty."

She very soon discovered that there is a charm about fine clothes which attracts a certain class of people. Several young ladies, who had taken no notice of her before, were very affectionate all of a sudden; several young gentlemen, who had only stared at her at the other party, asked to be introduced, and several old ladies inquired who she was with an air of interest. She heard Mrs. Moffat reply to one of them, — "Daisy March — father a colonel in the army — one of our first families, but reverses of fortune, you know; intimate friends of the Laurences; sweet creature, I assure you; my Ned is quite wild about her."

The "queer feeling" did not pass away, but she imagined herself acting the new part of fine lady, and so got on pretty well, though the tight dress gave her a side-ache, the train kept getting under her feet, and she was in constant fear lest her ear-rings should fly off. She was flirting her fan, and laughing at the feeble jokes of a young gentleman who tried to be witty, when she suddenly stopped laughing, and looked confused, for, just opposite, she saw Laurie. He was staring at her with surprise and disapproval also, she thought; for though he bowed and smiled, yet something in his honest eyes made her blush, and wish she had her old dress on. She saw Belle nudge Annie, and both glance from her to Laurie.

"Silly creatures, to put such thoughts into my head! I won't care for it, or let it change me a bit," thought Meg, and rustled across the room to shake hands with her friend.

"I am glad you came, for I was afraid you wouldn't," she said, with her most grown-up air.

"Jo wanted me to come, and tell her how you looked, so I did," answered Laurie.

"What shall you tell her?" asked Meg, full of curiosity to know his opinion of her.

"I shall say I didn't know you, for you look so grown-up, and unlike yourself; I'm quite afraid of you," he said fumbling at his glove-button.

"How absurd of you! the girls dressed me up for fun, and I rather like it. Wouldn't Jo stare if she saw me?"

"Yes, I think she would," returned Laurie gravely.

"Don't you like me so?" asked Meg.

"No, I don't," was the blunt reply.

"Why not?" in an anxious tone.

He glanced at her frizzled head, bare shoulders, and fantastically trimmed dress with an expression that abashed her more than his answer, which had not a particle of his usual politeness about it: — "I don't like fuss and feathers."

That was altogether too much from a lad younger than herself; and Meg walked away, saying petulantly, — "You are the rudest boy I ever saw."

Feeling much ruffled, she went and stood at a quiet window, to cool her cheeks. As she stood there, Major Lincoln passed by; and she heard him saying to his mother, — "They are making a fool of that little girl; I wanted you to see her, but they have spoilt her entirely; she's nothing but a doll tonight."

She leaned her forehead on the cool pane, and stood half hidden by the curtains; and turning, she saw Laurie looking penitent, as he said, "Please forgive my rudeness, and come and dance with me."

"I'm afraid it will be too disagreeable to you," said Meg, trying to look offended.

"Not a bit of it; I'm dying to do it. Come, I'll be good; I don't like your gown, but I do think you are just splendid"; and he waved his hands, as if words failed to express his admiration.

Meg smiled, and relented, and whispered as they stood waiting to catch the time: "Take care my skirt doesn't trip you up; it's the plague of my life, and I was a goose to wear it."

Away they went, fleetly and gracefully; for, having practised at home, they were well matched, and the blithe young couple were a pleasant sight to see, as they twirled merrily round and round, feeling more friendly than ever after their tiff.

"Laurie, I want you to do me a favour, will you?" said Meg, as he stood fanning her, when her breath gave out.

"Won't I !" said Laurie with alacrity.

"Please don't tell them at home about my dress tonight. They won't understand the joke, and it will worry mother."

"Then why did you do it?" said Laurie's eyes, so plainly that Meg hastily added:

"I shall tell them, myself, all about it, and 'fess' to mother how silly I've been. But I'd rather do it myself; so you'll not tell, will you?"

"I give you my word I won't. Here comes Ned Moffat; what does he want?" said Laurie, knitting his black brows.

"He put his name down for three dances, and I suppose he's coming for them; what a bore!" said Meg, assuming a languid air, which amused Laurie immensely.

He did not speak to her again until supper time, when he saw her drinking champagne with Ned and his friend Fisher, who were behaving "like a pair of fools," as Laurie said to himself.

"You'll have a splitting headache tomorrow if you drink much of that. I wouldn't, Meg: your mother doesn't like it, you know," he whispered.

"I'm not Meg tonight; I'm a 'doll,' who does all sorts of crazy things. Tomorow I shall put away my 'fuss and feathers,' and be good again."

"Wish tomorrow was here, then," muttered Laurie, walking off.

Meg danced and flirted, chattered and giggled, as the other girls did, romping in a way that scandalized Laurie, who looked on and meditated a lecture. But he got no chance to deliver it, for Meg kept away from him till he came to say good night.

"Remember!" she said, trying to smile, for the splitting headache had already begun.

"Silence *à la mort*," replied Laurie, with a melodramatic flourish, as he went away.

This little bit of by-play excited Annie's curiosity; but Meg was too tired for gossip, and went to bed feeling as if she had been to a masquerade. She was sick all the next day, and on Saturday went home, quite used up with her fortnight's fun.

"Home *is* a nice place, though it isn't splendid," said Meg, looking about her with a restful expression, as she sat with her mother and Jo on the Sunday evening.

"I'm glad to hear you say so, dear, for I was afraid home would seem dull and poor to you, after your fine quarters," replied her mother, who had given her many anxious looks that day.

Meg had told her adventures gaily, and said what a charming time she had had; but something still seemed to weigh upon her spirits, and, when the younger girls were gone to bed, she sat staring at the fire, saying little, and looking worried. As the clock struck nine, and Jo proposed bed, Meg suddenly left her chair, and, taking Beth's stool, leaned her elbows on her mother's knee, saying bravely, —

"Marmee, I want to 'fess'."

"I thought so; what is it, dear?"

"Shall I go away?" asked Jo discreetly.

"Of course not. I was ashamed to speak of it before the children, but I want you to know all the dreadful things I did at the Moffats."

"We are prepared," said Mrs. March, smiling.

"I told you they rigged me up, but I didn't tell you that they powdered, and squeezed, and frizzled, and made me look like a fashion plate. Laurie thought I wasn't proper; and one man called me 'a doll'."

"Is that all?" asked Jo.

"No; I drank champagne, and romped, and tried to flirt, and was altogether abominable."

"There is something more, I think"; and Mrs. March smoothed the soft cheek, which suddenly grew rosy, as Meg answered slowly —

"Yes; it's very silly, but I want to tell it, because I hate to have people say and think such things about us and Laurie."

Then she told the various bits of gossip she had heard at the Moffats'; and, as she spoke, Jo saw her mother fold her lips tightly.

"Well, if that isn't the greatest rubbish I ever heard," cried Jo indignantly. "Just wait till I see Annie Moffat, and I'll show you how to settle such ridiculous stuff. The idea of having 'plans', and being kind to Laurie because he's rich, and may marry us by-and-by! Won't he shout when I tell him what those silly things say about us!"

"If you tell Laurie, I'll never forgive you! She mustn't, must she, mother?" said Meg, looking distressed.

"No; never repeat that foolish gossip, and forget it as soon as you can," said Mrs. March gravely. "I was very unwise to let you go among people of whom I know so little; kind, I say, but worldly, and full of these vulgar ideas about young people. I am sorry for the mischief this visit may have done you, Meg."

"Don't be sorry; I'll forget all the bad, and remember only the good; for I did enjoy a great deal. I'll not be sentimental or dissatisfied, mother. But it is nice to be praised and admired, and I can't help saying I like it," said Meg.

"That is perfectly natural and quite harmless, if the liking does not become a passion, and lead one to do foolish things. Learn to value the praise which is worth having, and to excite the admiration of excellent people, by being modest as well as pretty, Meg."

Jo stood with her hands behind her, looking perplexed; for it was a new thing to see Meg blushing and talking about admiration, and Jo felt as if her sister had grown up, and was drifting away from her into a world where she could not follow.

"Mother, do you have 'plans', as Mrs. Moffat said?" asked Meg bashfully.

"Yes, my dear, all mothers do. I *am* ambitious for you; but not to marry rich men merely because they are rich. I'd rather see you poor men's wives, if you were happy, than queens on thrones, without self-respect and peace."

"Poor girls don't stand any chance, Belle says," sighed Meg.

"Then we'll be old maids," said Jo stoutly.

"Right, Jo, better be happy old maids than unhappy wives," said Mrs. March decidedly. "Don't be troubled, Meg; poverty seldom daunts a sincere lover. One thing remember, my girls, mother is always ready to be your confidante, father to be your friend; and both of us trust that our daughters, whether married or single, will be the pride and comfort of our lives."

"We will, Marmee, we will!" cried both, with all their hearts, as she bade them good night.

CHAPTER TEN

# THE P.C. AND P,O.

As spring came on, a new set of amusements became the fashion. Gardening, walks, rows on the river, and flower-hunts employed the fine days; and for rainy ones they had house diversions. One of these was the "P.C."; for as secret societies were the fashion, it was thought proper to have one; and as all the girls admired Dickens, they called themselves the Pickwick Club. They met every Saturday evening in the big garret. Three chairs were arranged in a row before a table, on which was a lamp, also four white badges, with a big "P.C." in different colours on each, and the weekly newspaper, called the *Pickwick Portfolio,* to which all contributed something; while Jo, who revelled in pens and ink, was the editor. At seven o'clock the four members ascended to the club-room, tied their badges round their heads, and took their seats with great solemnity. Meg, as the eldest, was Samuel Pickwick; Jo, being of a literary turn, Augustus Snodgrass; Beth, because she was round and rosy, Tracy Tupman; and Amy, who was always trying to do what she couldn't, was Nathaniel Winkle. Pickwick, the president, read the paper, which was filled with original tales, poetry, local news, funny advertisements, and hints, in which they good-naturedly reminded each other of their faults and short-comings.

As the President finished reading the paper a round of applause followed, and then Mr. Snodgrass rose to make a proposition.

"Mr. President and gentlemen," he began, "I wish to propose the admission of a new member. I propose Mr. Theodore Laurence as an honorary member of the P.C."

"We'll put it to vote," said the President." All in favour of this motion please to manifest it by saying 'Ay'."

A loud response from Snodgrass, followed, to everybody's surprise, by a timid one from Beth.

"Contrary-minded say 'No'."

Meg and Amy were contrary minded; and Mr. Winkle rose to say, "We don't want any boys. This is a ladies' club."

"I'm afraid he'll laugh at our paper, and make fun of us afterwards," observed Pickwick, pulling the little curl on her forehead.

Up bounded Snodgrass.

"Sir ! I give you my word as a gentleman, Laurie won't do anything of the sort. We can do so little for him, and he does so much for us, I think the least we can do is to offer him a place here, and make him welcome."

This artful allusion to benefits conferred brought Tupman to his feet.

"Yes; we ought to do it, even if we are afraid. I say he may come, and his grandpa too, if he likes."

This spirited burst from Beth electrified the club, and Jo left her seat to shake hands approvingly. "Now then, vote again. Everybody remember it's our Laurie, and say 'Ay' !" cried Snodgrass excitely.

"Ay! ay! ay!" replied three voices at once.

"Good ! bless you ! Now, as there's nothing like 'taking time by the fetlock,' as Winkle observes, allow me to present the new member"; and, to the dismay of the rest of the club, Jo threw open the door of the closet, and displayed Laurie sitting on a rag-bag, flushed and twinkling with suppressed laughter.

"You rogue ! you traitor ! Jo, how could you?" cried the three girls, as Snodgrass led her friend triumphantly forth; and producing both a chair and a badge, installed him in a jiffy.

"The coolness of you two rascals is amazing," began Mr. Pickwick, trying to get up an awful frown. But the new member was equal to the occasion; and, rising with a graceful salutation to the chair, said: — "Mr. President and ladies — I beg your pardon, gentlemen — allow me to introduce myself as Sam Weller, the very humble servant of the club."

"Good, good !" cried Jo, pounding with the handle of the old warming-pan on which she leaned.

"My faithful friend and noble patron," continued Laurie with a wave of the hand, "who has so flatteringly presented me is not to be blamed for the base stratagem of tonight. I planned it."

"Come, now, don't lay it all on yourself; you know I proposed the cupboard," broke in Snodgrass.

"Never you mind what she says. I'm the wretch that did it sir," said the new member. "But on my honour, I never will do so again, and henceforth devote myself to the interest of this immortal club."

"Hear ! hear !" cried Jo, clashing the lid of the warming-pan like a cymbal.

"As a token of my gratitude for the honour done me, and as a means of promoting friendly relations between adjoining nations, I have set up a post office in the hedge in the lower corner of the garden; a fine, spacious building, with padlocks on the doors, and every convenience for the mails — also the females. It's the old martin-house; but I've stopped up the door, and made the roof open, so it will hold all sorts of things, and save our valuable time. Letters, manuscripts, books and bundles can be passed in there; and as each nation has a key, it will be uncommonly nice, I fancy. Allow me to present the club key."

No one ever regretted the admittance of Sam Weller; for a more devoted, well-behaved, and jovial member no club could have. His orations convulsed his hearers, and his contributions were excellent, being patriotic, classical, comical, or dramatic.

The P.O. was a capital little institution, and flourished wonderfully; for nearly as many queer things passed through it as through the real office. Tragedies and cravats, poetry and pickles, garden seeds and long letters, music and gingerbread, rubbers, invitations, scoldings, and puppies. The old gentleman liked the fun, amused himself by sending odd bundles, mysterious messages, and funny telegrams; and his gardener, who was smitten with Hannah's charms, actually sent a love-letter to Jo's care. How they laughed when the secret came out, never dreaming how many love-letters that little post-office would hold in the years to come !

CHAPTER ELEVEN

## EXPERIMENTS

"THE FIRST OF JUNE; the Kings are off to the seashore tomorrow, and I'm free ! Three months' vacation ! how I shall enjoy it!" exclaimed Meg, coming home one warm day to find Jo laid upon the sofa in an unusual state of exhaustion, while Beth took off her dusty boots, and Amy made lemonade for the refreshment of the whole party.

"What shall you do all your vacation ?" said Amy.

"I shall lie a-bed late, and do nothing," replied Meg, from the depths of the rocking-chair. "I've been routed up early all winter, and had to spend my days working for other people, so now I'm going to rest and revel to my heart's content."

"Hum!" said Jo; "that dozy way wouldn't suit me. I've laid in a heap of books, and I'm going to improve my shining hours reading on my perch in the old apple-tree."

"Don't let us do any lessons, Beth, for a while, but play all the time, and rest, as the girls mean to," proposed Amy.

"Well, I will, if mother don't mind. I want to learn some new songs, and my children need fixing up for the summer; they are dreadfully out of order, and really suffering for clothes."

"May we mother?" asked Meg, turning to Mrs. March, who sat sewing in what they called "Marmee's corner."

"You may try your experiment for a week .I think by Saturday night you will find that all play and no work is as bad as all work and no play."

"Oh, dear, no! it will be delicious. I'm sure," said Meg complacently.

Next morning, Meg did not appear till ten o'clock; her solitary breakfast did not taste good, and the room seemed lonely and untidy, for Jo had not filled the vases, Beth had not dusted, and Amy's books lay scattered about. Nothing was neat and pleasant but "Marmee's corner," which looked as usual; and there she sat to "rest and read," which meant yawn, and imagine what pretty summer dresses she could get with her salary. Jo spent the morning on the river with Laurie, and the afternoon reading and crying over *The Wide, Wide World* up in the apple-tree. Beth began by rummaging everything out of the big closet, where her family resided; getting tired before half done, she left her establishment topsy-turvy, and went to her music, rejoicing that she had no dishes to wash. Amy arranged her bower, put on her best white frock, smoothed her curls, and sat down to draw, under the honeysuckle; hoping someone would see and inquire who the young artist was. As no one appeared but an inquisitive daddy-long-legs, she went to walk, got caught in a shower, and came home dripping.

At tea-time they compared notes, and all agreed that it had been a delightful though unusually long day. Meg, who went shopping in the afternoon, and got a "sweet blue muslin," had discovered after she had cut the breadths off, that it wouldn't wash, which mishap made her sligthly cross. Jo had burnt the skin off her nose boating, and got a raging headache by reading too long. Beth was worried by the confusion of her closet; and Amy regretted the damage done to her frock, for Katy Brown's party was to be the next day; and now she had nothing to wear. But these were mere trifles, and they assured their mother that the experiment was working finely. She smiled, said nothing, and, with Hannah's help, did their neglected work. It was astonishing what a peculiar state of things was produced by the "resting and revelling" process. The days kept getting longer; the weather was variable, and so were tempers; an unsettled feeling possessed everyone, and Satan found mischief for the idle hands to do. As the height of luxury, Meg put out some of her sewing, and then found time hang so heavily that she fell to snipping and spoiling her clothes in her attempts to furbish them up, *à la* Moffat. Jo read till her eyes gave out, and she was sick of books, and got so fidgety that even Laurie had a quarrel with her. Beth got on pretty well, for she was constantly forgetting that it was to be *all play and no work,* and fell back into her old ways, now and then; but something in the air affected her, and, more than once, her tranquillity was disturbed; so much so that, on one occasion, she actually shook poor dear Joanna, and told her she was "a fright." Amy fared worst of all, for her resources were small. She didn't like dolls; fairy tales were childish, and one couldn't draw all the time. "If one could have a fine house, full of nice girls, or go travelling, the summer would be delightful; but to stay at home with three selfish sisters and a grown-up boy was enough to try the patience of a Boaz," complained Miss Malaprop, after several days devoted to pleasure, fretting, and *ennui*.

No one would own that they were tired of the experiment; but, by Friday night, each acknowledged to herself that they were glad the week was nearly done. Hoping to impress the lesson more deeply, Mrs. March, who had a good deal of humour, resolved to finish off the trial in an appropriate manner, so she gave Hannah a holiday.

When they got up on Saturday morning there was no fire in the kitchen, no breakfast in the dining-room, and no mother anywhere to be seen.

"Mercy on us! what *has* happened?" cried Jo.

Meg ran upstairs, and soon came back again, looking relieved, but rather bewildered.

"Mother isn't sick, only very tired; and she says she is going to stay quietly in her room all day, and let us do the best we can."

"That's easy enough, and I like the idea; I'm aching for something to do — that is, some new amusement, you know," added Jo quickly.

In fact, it *was* an immense relief to them all to have a little work, and they took hold with a will, but soon realised the truth of Hannah's saying, "Housekeeping ain't no joke." There was plenty of food in the larder, and, while Beth and Amy set the table, Meg and Jo got breakfast.

"I shall take some up to mother, though she said we were not to think of her, for she'd take care of herself," said Meg.

So a tray was fitted out before anyone began, and taken up, with the cook's compliments. The boiled tea was very bitter, the omelette scorched; but Mrs. March received her repast with thanks, and laughed heartily over it after Jo was gone.

Many were the complaints below, and great the chagrin of the head cook, at her failures. "Never mind, I'll get the dinner and be servant; you be missus, keep your hands nice, see company, and give orders," said Jo.

This offer was gladly accepted, and Margaret retired to the parlour, which she put hastily in order by whisking the litter under the sofa, and shutting the blinds to save the trouble of dusting. Jo, with perfect faith in her own powers, and a friendly desire to make up the quarrel, put a note in the office inviting Laurie to dinner.

"You'd better see what you have got before you think of having company," said Meg.

"Oh, there's corned beef, and plenty of potatoes; and I shall get some asparagus, and a lobster, 'for a relish,' as Hannah says. We'll have lettuce, and make a salad. I'll have blanc-mange and strawberries for dessert; and coffee, too."

"Get what you like. I'm going out to dinner," said Mrs. March, when Jo spoke to her.

The unusual spectacle of her busy mother rocking comfortably, and reading early in the morning made Jo feel as if some natural phenomenon had occurred; for an eclipse, or a volcanic eruption would hardly have seemed stranger.

"Everything is out of sorts, somehow," she said to herself going downstairs. "There's Beth crying; that's a sure sign that something is wrong with this family."

Jo hurried into the parlour, to find Beth sobbing over Pip, the canary, who lay dead in the cage, with his little claws, pathetically extended, as if imploring the food for want of which he had died.

"It's all my fault — I forgot him — there isn't a seed or drop left — oh, Pip! oh, Pip! How could I be so cruel to you!" cried Beth, taking the poor thing in her hands, and trying to restore him.

Jo peeped into his half-open eye, felt his little heart, and finding him stiff and cold, shook her head, and offered her domino-box for a coffin.

"The funeral shall be this afternoon, and we will all go. Now, don't cry, Bethy; it's a pity, but nothing goes right this week, and Pip has had the worst of the experiment. Make the shroud, and lay him in my box; and, after the dinner-party, we'll have a nice little funeral," said Jo.

Leaving the others to console Beth, she departed to the kitchen, which was in a most discouraging state of confusion. Putting on a big apron, she fell to work, and got the dishes piled up ready for washing, when she discovered that the fire was out.

"Here's a sweet prospect!" muttered Jo, slamming the stove door open, and poking among the cinders.

Having re-kindled it, she thought she would go to market while the water heated. The walk revived her spirits; and, flattering herself she had made good bargains, she trudged home again, after buying a very young lobster, some very old asparagus and two boxes of acid strawberries. By the time she had got cleared up, the dinner arrived, and the stove was red-hot. Hannah had left a pan of bread to rise, Meg had worked it up early, set it on the hearth for a second rising, and forgotten it. Meg was entertaining Sallie Gardiner, in the parlour, when the door flew open, and a floury, and dishevelled figure appeared, demanding tartly, — "I say, isn't bread 'riz' enough when it runs over the pans?"

Sallie began to laugh; but Meg nodded, and lifted her eyebrows as high as they would go, which caused the apparition to vanish, and put the sour bead into the oven without further delay. Mrs. March went out, after saying a word of comfort to Beth, who sat making a winding-sheet, while the dear-departed lay in the domino-box. A strange sense of helplessness fell upon the girls as the grey bonnet vanished round the corner; and despair seized them when, a few minutes later, Miss Crocker appeared, and said she'd come to dinner. Now this lady was a thin spinster, with a sharp nose and inquisitive eyes, who saw everything, and gossiped about all she saw. They disliked her, but had been taught to be kind to her, simply because she was old and poor, and had few friends. So Meg gave her the easy-chair, and tried to entertain her, while she asked questions, criticised everything, and told stories of the people whom she knew.

Language cannot describe the anxieties, and exertions which Jo underwent that morning; and the dinner she served up became a standing joke. Fearing to ask more advice, she did her best alone. She boiled the asparagus hard for an hour, and was grieved to find the heads burnt off, and the stalks harder than ever. The bread burnt black; for the salad dressing so aggravated her that she let everything else go, till she had convinced herself that she could not make it fit to eat. The lobster was a great mystery to her, but she hammered and poked, till it was unshelled, and its meagre proportions concealed in a grove of lettuce leaves. The potatoes had to be hurried, not to keep the asparagus waiting, and were not done at last. The blanc-mange was lumpy, and the strawberries not as ripe as they looked.

"Well, they can eat beef and bread and butter, if they are hungry; only it's mortifying to have to spend your whole morning for nothing," thought Jo, so she rang the bell half an hour later than usual, and stood, hot, tired, and dispirited, surveying the feast spread for Laurie, accustomed to all sorts of elegance, and Miss Crocker, whose curious eyes would mark all failures, and whose tattling tongue would report them far and wide.

Poor Jo would have gladly gone under the table, as one thing after another was tasted and left; while Amy giggled, Meg looked distressed, Miss Crocker pursed up her lips, and Laurie talked and laughed with all his might, to give a cheerful tone to this festive scene. Jo's one strong point was the fruit, for she had sugared it well, and had a pitcher of rich cream to eat with it. Her hot cheeks cooled a trifle, and she drew a long breath, as the pretty glass plates went round, and everyone looked graciously at the little rosy islands floating in a sea of cream. Miss Crocker tasted first, made a wry face, and drank some water hastily. Jo who had refused thinking there might not be enough, glanced at Laurie, but he was eating away manfully, though there was a slight pucker about his mouth, and he kept his eye fixed on his plate. Amy, who was fond of delicate fare, took a heaping spoonful, choked, hid her face in her napkin, and left the table precipitately.

"Oh, what is it ?" exclaimed Jo, trembling.

"Salt instead of sugar, and the cream is sour," replied Meg, with a tragic gesture.

Jo uttered a groan, and fell back in her chair, remembering that she had given a last hasty powdering to the berries out of one of the two boxes on the kitchen table, and had neglected to put the milk in the refrigerator. She turned scarlet, and was on the verge of crying, when she met Laurie's eyes, which *would* look merry, in spite of his heroic efforts; the comical side of the affair suddenly struck her, and she laughed till the tears ran down her cheeks. So did everyone else, even "Croaker" as the girls called the old lady, and the unfortunate dinner ended gaily, with bread and butter, olives and fun.

"I haven't strength of mind enough to clear up now, so we will sober ourselves with a funeral," said Jo, as they rose; and Miss Crocker made ready to go, being eager to tell the new story at another friend's dinner table.

They did sober themselves, for Beth's sake; Laurie dug a grave under the ferns in the grove, little Pip was laid in, with many tears, by his tender-hearted mistress, and covered with moss, while a wreath of violets and chickweed was hung on the stone which bore his epitaph, composed by Jo, while she struggled with the dinner:

> "Here lies Pip March,
>     Who died the 7th of June;
> Loved and lamented sore,
>     And not forgotten soon."

At the conclusion of the ceremonies, Beth retired to her room overcome with emotion and lobster; but there was no place of repose, for the beds were not made, and she found her grief much assuaged by beating up pillows and putting things in order. Meg helped Jo clear away the remains of the feast, which took half the afternoon, and left them so tired that they agreed to be contented with tea and toast for supper. Laurie took Amy to drive, which was a deed of charity, for the sour cream seemed to have had a bad effect upon her temper. Mrs. March came home to find the three older girls hard at work in the middle of the afternoon; and a glance at the closet gave her an idea of the success of one part of the experiment.

Before the housewives could rest, several people called and there was a scramble to get ready to see them; then tea must be got, errands done and one or two bits of sewing were necessary, but neglected till the last minute. As twilight fell, one by one they gathered in the porch.

"What a dreadful day this has been !" began Jo.

"It has seemed shorter than usual, but so uncomfortable," said Meg.

"Not a bit like home," added Amy.

"It can't seem so without Marmee and little Pip," sighed Beth.

"Here's mother, dear; and you shall have another bird tomorrow, if you want it."

As she spoke, Mrs. March came and took her place among them.

"Are you satisfied with your experiment, girls, or do you want another week of it ?" she asked.

"I don't ! cried Jo decidedly.

"Nor I," echoed the others.

"Lounging and larking don't pay," observed Jo, shaking her head. "I'm tired of it, and mean to go to work at something right off."

"Suppose you learn plain cooking; that's a useful accomplishment, which no woman should be without," said Mrs. March, laughing at the recollection of Jo's dinner-party; for she had met Miss Crocker, and heard her account of it.

"Mother! did you go away and let everything be, just to see how we'd get on ?" cried Meg.

"Yes; I wanted you to see how the comfort of all depends on each doing her share faithfully. While Hannah and I did your work, you got on pretty well, though I don't think you were very happy or amiable; so I thought, as a little lesson, I would show you what happens when everyone thinks only of herself. Don't you feel that it is pleasanter to help one another, to have daily duties which make leisure sweet when it comes, and to bear or forbear, that home may be comfortable and lovely to us all ?"

"We do, mother, we do !" cried the girls.

"Then let me advise you to take up your little burdens again; for, though they seem heavy sometimes, they are good for us and lighten as we learn to carry them. Work is wholesome, and there is plenty for everyone."

"We'll work like bees, and love it too; see if we don't !" said Jo. "I'll learn plain cooking for my holiday task; and the next dinner-party I have shall be a success."

"I'll make the sets of shirts for father, instead of letting you do it, Marmee. That will be better than fussing over my own things," said Meg.

"I'll do my lessons every day, and not spend so much time with my music and dolls. I am a stupid thing, and ought to be studying, not playing," was Beth's resolution; while Amy followed their example by heroically declaring: "I shall learn to make button-holes, and attend to my parts of speech."

"Very good! Then I am quite satisfied with the experiment."

CHAPTER TWELVE

# CAMP LAURENCE

Beth was post-mistress, and dearly liked the daily task of unlocking the little door and distributing the mail. One July day, she came in with her hands full, and went about the house leaving letters and parcels like the penny post.

"Here's your posy, mother ! Laurie never forgets that," she said, putting the fresh nosegay in the wase that stood in "Marmee's corner."

"Miss Meg March, one letter and a glove," continued Beth.

"Why, I left a pair over there, and here is only one," said Meg, looking at the grey cotton glove.

"I hate to have odd gloves ! Never mind, the other may be found. My letter is only a translation of the German song I wanted; I guess Mr. Brooke did it, for this is not Laurie's writing."

Mrs. March glanced at Meg, who was looking very pretty in her gingham morning-gown, with the little curls blowing about her forehead, and very womanly as she sat sewing at her little work-table.

"Two letters for Doctor Jo, a book and a funny old hat," said Beth, laughing, as she went into the study, where Jo sat writing.

"What a sly fellow Laurie is ! I said I wished bigger hats were the fashion, because I burn my face every hot day. He said, 'Why mind the fashion? Wear a big hat, and be comfortable !' I said I would, if I had one, and he has sent me this to wear to try me; I'll wear it for fun, and show him I *don't* care for the fashion" and, hanging the antique broad-brim on a bust of Plato, Jo read her letters.

One from her mother made her cheeks glow and her eyes fill, for it said to her, —

"MY DEAR, — I write a little word to tell you with how much satisfaction I watch your efforts to control your temper. Go on, dear, patiently and bravely, and always believe that no one sympathises more tenderly with you that your loving

MOTHER"

"That does me good! that's worth millions of money, and pecks of praise. Oh, Marmee, I do try! I will keep on trying and not get tired, since I have you to help me."

Laying her head on her arms, Jo wet her romance with a few happy tears, for she had thought no one saw and appreciated her efforts to be good. Feeling stronger than ever to meet her Apollyon, she proceeded to open her other letter. In a big, dashing hand, Laurie wrote, —

*"Dear Jo,*
*What ho !*

Some English girls and boys are coming to see me tomorrow. If it's fine, I'm going to pitch my tent in Longmeadow, and row up the whole crew to lunch and croquet; — have a fire ,make messes, gipsy fashion, and all sorts of larks. Brooke will go, to keep us boys steady, and Kate Vaughan will play propriety for the girls. I want you all to come; can't let Beth off at any price, and nobody shall worry her. Don't bother about rations — I'll see to that, and everything else — only do come, there's a good fellow !

*In a tearing hurry,*
*Yours ever, LAURIE."*

"Here's richness !" cried Jo, flying in to tell the news to Meg. "Of course we can go, mother; it will be such a help to Laurie, for I can row, and Meg see to the lunch, and the children be useful some way."

"I hope the Vaughans are not fine, grown-up people. Do you know anything about them, Jo?" asked Meg.

"Only that there are four of them. Kate is older than you, Fred and Frank (twins) about my age, and a little girl (Grace), who is nine or ten. Laurie knew them abroad, and liked the boys; I fancied that he did not admire Kate much."

"I'm so glad my French print is clean, it's just the thing, and so becoming !" observed Meg complacently. "Have you anything decent, Jo?"

"Scarlet and grey boating suit, good enough for me; I shall row and tramp about, so I don't want any starch to think of. You'll come, Bethy?"

"If you won't let any of the boys talk to me."

"Not a boy !"

"I like to please Laurie; and I'm not afraid of Mr. Brooke. He is so kind. But I don't want to play, or sing, or say anything. I'll work hard, and not trouble anyone; and you'll take care of me, Jo, so I'll go."

"That's my good girl; you do try to fight off you shyness, and I love you for it; fighting faults isn't easy, and a cheery kind of word gives a lift. Thank you, mother, and Jo gave the thin cheek a grateful kiss.

"I had a box of chocolate drops, and the picture I wanted to copy," said Amy, showing her mail.

"And I got a note from Mr. Laurence, asking me to come over and play to him to-night, before the lamps are lighted; and I shall go," added Beth, whose friendship with the old gentleman prospered finely.

When the sun peeped into the girls' room early next morning, he saw a comical sight. Each had made preparations for the fête. Meg had an extra row of little curl-papers across her forehead. Jo had anointed her afflicted face with cold cream. Beth had taken Joanna to bed with her to atone for the approaching separation, and Amy had put a clothes pin on her nose, to uplift the offending feature.

Sunshine and laughter were good omens for a pleasure party, and soon a lively bustle began in both houses, Beth reporting what went on next door.

"There goes the man with the tent! I see Mrs. Barker doing up the lunch in a hamper. Now Mr. Laurence is looking up to the sky and the weathercock; I wish he would go, too! There's Laurie, looking like a sailor — nice boy! Oh, mercy me! Here's a carriage full of people — a tall lady, a little girl and two dreadful boys. One is lame. Poor thing, he's got a crutch! Be quick, girls; it's getting late. Why, there is Ned Moffat, I do declare. Look, Meg; isn't that the man who bowed to you one day when we were shopping?"

"So it is; how queer that he should come! I thought he was at the Mountains. There is Sallie; I'm glad she got back in time. Am I all right, Jo?" cried Meg in a flutter.

"A regular daisy. Now then, come on."

"Oh, oh, Jo! You ain't going to wear that awful hat? You shall not make a guy of yourself," remonstrated Meg, as Jo tied down, with a red ribbon, the broad-brimmed, old-fashioned Leghorn Laurie had sent for a joke.

"I just will though. It's capital; so shady, light, and big. It will make fun; and I don't mind being a guy, if I'm comfortable." With that Jo marched straight away, and the rest followed: all looking their best in summer suits, with happy faces under their jaunty hat-brims.

Laurie ran to meet, and present them to his friends. The lawn was the reception-room and for several minutes a lively scene was enacted there. Meg was grateful to see Miss Kate, though twenty, was dressed with a simplicity which American girls would do well to imitate; and she was much flattered by Mr. Ned's assurance that the came especially to see her. Kate had a stand-off-don't-touch-me air, which contrasted strongly with the free-and-easy demeanour of the other girls. Beth took an observation of the new boys, and decided that the lame one was not "dreadful," but gentle and feeble, and she would be kind to him on that account. Amy found Grace a well-mannered, merry little person.

Tents, lunch and croquet utensils having been sent on before-hand, the party was soon embarked, and the two boats pushed off together. Laurie and Jo rowed one boat; Mr. Brooke and Ned the other. Jo's funny hat deserved a vote of thanks, for it broke the ice in the beginning by producing a laugh; it created a refreshing breeze, flapping to and fro as she rowed, and would make an excellent umbrella for the whole party if a shower came up, she said. Kate looked rather amazed at Jo's proceedings, especially as she exclaimed, "Christopher Columbus!" when she lost her oar; and Laurie said, "My dear fellow, did I hurt you?" when he tripped over her feet in taking his place. But, after putting up her glass to examine the queer girl several times, Miss Kate decided that she was "odd, but rather clever."

Meg, in the other boat, was delightfully situated — face to face with the rowers, who both admired the prospect. Mr. Brooke was a grave, silent young man, with handsome brown eyes and a pleasant voice. Meg liked his quiet manners, and considered him a walking encyclopaedia. He never talked to her much, but he looked at her a good deal. Ned being in college, put on all the airs which freshmen think it their bounden duty to assume; he was not very wise, but very good-natured and merry. Sallie Gardiner was absorbed in keeping her white pique dress clean, and chattering with Fred, who kept Beth in constant terror by his pranks.

It was not far to Longmeadow, but the tent was pitched and the wickets down by the time they arived. A pleasant green field, with three wide-spreading oaks in the middle, and a smooth strip of turf for croquet.

"Welcome to Camp Laurence!" said the young host as they landed. "Brooke is commander-in-chief; I am commissary general; the other fellows are staff-officers; and you ladies are company. The tent is for your special benefit, and that oak is your drawing-room; this is the mess-room and the third is the camp kitchen. Now let's have a game before it gets hot."

Frank, Beth, Amy and Grace sat down to watch the game. Mr. Brooke chose Meg, Kate, and Fred; Laurie took Sallie, Jo, and Ned. The Englishers played well, but the Americans played better. Jo and Fred had several skirmishes, and once narrowly escaped high words. Jo was through the last wicket and had missed the stroke, which failure ruffled her a good deal. Fred was close behind her, and his turn came before hers; he gave a stroke, his ball hit the wicket, and stopped an inch on the wrong side. No one was near and running up to examine, he gave it a nudge with his toe, which put it just an inch on the right side.

"I'm through! Now, Miss Jo, I'll settle you and get in first," cried the young gentleman.

"You pushed it! It's my turn now," said Jo sharply.

"Upon my word I didn't move it. It rolled a bit, perhaps, but that is allowed; so stand off, please, and let me have a go at the stake."

Jo opened her lips to say something rude, but checked herself in time, coloured up to her forehead, and stood a minute hammering down a wicket with all her might, while Fred hit the stake and declared himself out with much exultation. She went off to get her ball and was a long time finding it among the bushes; but she came back looking cool and quiet, and waited her turn patiently. It took several strokes to regain the place she had lost, and when she got there the other side had nearly won, for Kate's ball was the last one, and lay near the stake.

"By George, it's all up with us! Good-bye, Kate. Miss Jo owes me one, so you are finished, cried Fred excitedly.

"Yankees have a trick of being generous to their enemies," said Jo, with a look that made the lad redden, "especially when they beat them," she added, as, leaving Kate's ball untouched, she won the game by a clever stroke.

Laurie threw up his hat; then remembered that it wouldn't do to exult over the defeat of his guests, and stopped in the middle of a cheer to whisper to his friend, — "Good for you, Jo. He did cheat; I saw him. We can't tell him so; but he won't do it again, take my word for it."

Meg drew her aside, under pretence of pinning up a loose braid, and said approvingly, — "It was dreadfully provoking; but you kept your temper, and I'm so glad, Jo."

"Time for lunch," said Mr. Booke. "Commissary-general, will you make the fire and get water, while Miss March, Miss Sallie, and I spread the table. Who can make good coffee ?"

"Jo can," said Meg.

So Jo, feeling that her late lessons in cookery were to do her honour, went to preside over the coffee-pot, while the children collected sticks, and the boys made a fire and got water from a spring. Miss Kate sketched, and Frank talked to Beth, who was making little mats of braided rushes to serve as plates.

The commander-in-chief and his aides soon spread the tablecloth with an inviting array of eatables and drinkables, prettily decorated with green leaves. Jo announced that the coffee was ready, and everyone settled themselves to a hearty meal. A very merry lunch it was, for everything seemed fresh and funny, and frequently peals of laughter startled a venerable horse, who fed near by.

"There's salt here, if you prefer it," said Laurie, as he handed Jo a saucer of berries.

"Thank you, I prefer spiders," she replied, fishing up two unwary little ones, who had gone to a creamy death. "How dare you remind me of that horrid dinner party!"

"I had an uncommonly good time that day, and haven't got over it yet. This is no credit to me, you know; I don't do anything; it's you, and Meg, and Brooke who make it go, and I'm no end obliged to you. What shall we do when we can't eat any more?" asked Laurie.

Miss Kate did know several new games; and as the girls would not and the boys could not eat any more, they all adjourned to the drawing-room to play "Rigmarole."

"One person begins a story, and tells as long as they please, only taking care to stop at some exciting point, when the next takes it up. Please start it, Mr. Brooke," said Kate.

Lying on the grass, at the feet of the two young ladies, Mr. Brooke obediently began the story.

"Once on a time, a knight went out into the world to seek his fortune. He travelled a long while, till he came to the palace of a good old king, who had offered a reward to anyone who would tame a fine but unbroken colt. The knight agreed to try, and got on slowly, but surely. Every day, when he gave his lessons to this pet of the king's, the knight rode him through the city; and as he rode he looked everywhere for a certain beautiful face which he had seen many times in his dreams, but never found. One day, as he went prancing down a quiet street, he saw at the windows of a ruinous castle the lovely face. He was delighted, inquired who lived in this old castle, and was told that several captive princesses were kept there by a spell, and spun all day to lay up money to buy their liberty. The knight wished that he could free them; but he was poor, and could only go by each day watching for the sweet face. At last, he resolved to get into the castle, and ask how he could help them. He went and knocked; the great door flew open, and he beheld —"

"A ravishing lovely lady, who exclaimed with a cry of rapture, 'At last! at last!'" continued Kate, who had read French novels. "Tis she!' cried Count Gustave, and fell at her feet in an ecstasy of joy. 'Oh, rise!' she said, extending a hand of marble fairness. 'Never ! till you tell me how I may rescue you,' swore the knight, still kneeling. 'Alas, my cruel fate condemns me to remain here till my tyrant is destroyed.' 'Where is the villain ?' 'In the mauve salon; go, brave heart, and save me from despair.' 'I obey.' With these words he rushed away, and, flinging open the door of the mauve salon, was about to enter, when he received —"

"A stunning blow from the big Greek lexicon, which an old fellow in a black gown fired at him," said Ned. "Instantly Sir What's-his-name recovered himself, pitched the tyrant out of the window, and turned to join the lady, victorious, but with a bump on his brow; found the door locked, tore up the curtains, made a rope-ladder, got half-way down, when the ladder broke, and he went head first into the moat, sixty feet below. Could swim like a duck; paddled round the castle till he came to a little door, guarded by two stout fellows; knocked their heads together till they cracked open like a couple of nuts; then smashed in the door, went up a pair of stone steps covered with dust a foot thick, toads as big as your fist. At the top of these steps he came plump upon a sight that chilled his blood —"

"A tall figure, all in white, with a veil over its face, and a lamp in its wasted hand," went on Meg. "It beckoned, gliding noiselessly before him down a corridor as dark and cold as any tomb. Shadowy effigies in armour stood on either side, a dead silence reigned, the lamp burned blue, and the ghostly figure turned its face towards him, showing the glitter of awful eyes through its white veil. They reached a curtained door, behind which sounded lovely music; he sprang forward to enter, but the spectre plucked him back, and waved threateningly before him a —"

"Snuff-box," said Jo, in a sepulchral tone, which convulsed the audience. 'Thank'ee,' said the knight politely, as he took a pinch, and sneezed seven times so violently that his head fell off. 'Ha! ha!' laughed the ghost; and, having peeped through the keyhole at the princesses spinning away for dear life, the evil spirit picked up her victim and put him in a large tin box, where there were eleven other knights packed together without their heads, like sardines, who all rose and began to —"

"Dance a hornpipe," cut in Fred, and as they danced the rubbishy old castle turned to a man-of-war. 'Up with the jib, reef the tops'l halliards, helm hard a-lee, and man the guns,' roared the captain, as a Portuguese pirate hove in sight. 'Go in and win, my hearties,' says the captain; and a tremendous fight began. Of course the British beat — they always do; and, having taken the pirate captain prisoner, sailed slap over the schooner, whose decks were piled with dead, for the order had been 'Cutlasses, and die hard.' 'Bosen's mate, take a bight of the flying jib sheet, and start this villain if he don't confess his sins double quick,' said the British captain. The Portuguese held his tongue like a brick, and walked the plank. But the sly dog dived, came up under the man-of-war, scuttled her, and down she went, with all sail set, where —"

"Oh, gracious! what shall I say?" cried Sallie, as Fred ended his rigmarole. "Well, they went to the bottom, and a nice mermaid welcomed them, but was much grieved on finding a box of headless knights, and kindly pickled them in brine. By-and-by a diver came down, and the mermaid said, 'I'll give you this box of pearls if you can take it up; for she wanted to restore the poor things to life. So the diver hoisted it up, and was much disappointed on opening it, to find no pearls. He left it in a great lonely field, where it was found by a —"

"Little goose-girl, who kept a hundred fat geese in the field,' said Amy. "The little girl was sorry for them, and asked an old woman what she should do to help them. 'Your geese will tell you; they know everything," said the old woman. So she asked what she should use for new heads, and all the geese opened their hundred mouths, and screamed —"

"Cabbages!" continued Laurie promptly. "'Just the thing,' said the girl, and ran to get twelve fine ones from her garden.

She put them on, the knights revived at once, thanked her, and went on their way rejoicing, never knowing the difference, for there were so many other heads like them in the world. The knight went back to find the pretty face, and learned that the princesses had spun themselves free, and all gone to be married but one. He was in a great state of mind at that; and, mounting the colt, rushed to the castle to see which was left. Peeping over the hedge, he saw the queen of his affections picking flowers. 'Will you give me a rose?' said he. 'You must come and get it,' said she. He tried to climb over the hedge, but it seemed to grow higher and higher; then he tried to push through but it grew thicker and thicker. So he patiently broke twig after twig, till he had made a little hole, through which he peeped, saying imploringly, 'Let me in! let me in!' But the pretty princess left him to fight his way in. Whether he did or not, Frank will tell you."

"I can't; I'm not playing, I never do," said Frank, dismayed at the sentimental predicament out of which he was to rescue the absurd couple. Beth had disappeared behind Jo, and Grace was asleep.

"So the poor knight is to be left sticking in the hedge, is he?" asked Mr. Brooke.

"I guess the princess gave him a posy, and opened the gate, after a while," said Laurie, smiling to himself, as he threw acorns at his tutor.

"Let's have a sensible game of Authors, to refresh our minds," proposed Jo.

Ned, Frank, and the little girls joined in this, and, while it went on, the three elders sat apart, talking. Miss Kate took out her sketch again, and Margaret watched her, while Mr. Brooke lay on the grass with a book which he did not read.

"How beautifully you do it! I wish I could draw," said Meg.

"Why don't you learn? I should think you had taste and talent for it," replied Kate.

"I haven't time."

"Your mamma prefers other accomplishments, I fancy. So did mine; but I proved to her that I had talent by taking a few lessons privately, and then she was quite willing I should go on. Can't you do the same with your governess?"

"I have none."

"I forgot; young ladies in America go to school more than with us. Very fine schools they are too, papa says. You go to a private one, I suppose?"

"I don't go at all; I am a governess myself."

"Oh indeed!" said Miss Kate; but she might as well have said, "Dear me, how dreadful!" for her tone implied it, and something in her face made Meg colour.

Mr. Brooke looked up, and said quickly, "Young ladies in America love independence as much as their ancestors did, and are admired and respected for supporting themselves."

"Oh yes; of course! It's very nice and proper in them to do so."

"Did the German song suit, Miss March?" inquired Mr. Brooke, breaking an awkward pause.

"Oh yes! it was very sweet, and I'm much obliged to who ever translated it for me"; and Meg's downcast face brightened as she spoke.

"Don't you read German?" asked Miss Kate.

"Not very well. My father, who taught me, is away, and I don't get on very fast alone."

"Try a little now; here is Schiller's Mary Stuart, and a tutor who loves to teach"; and Mr. Brooke laid his book on her lap with an inviting smile.

"It's so hard, I'm afraid to try," said Meg.

"I'll read a bit to encourage you," said Miss Kate and she read one of the most beautiful passages, in a correct, but expressionless manner.

Mr. Brooke made no comment, as she returned the book to Meg, who said innocently, —

"I thought it was poetry."

"Some of it is; try this passage."

There was a queer smile about Mr. Brooke's mouth as he opened it at poor Mary's lament.

Meg, obediently following the long grass blade which her new tutor used to point with, read slowly and timidly, unconsciously making poetry of the hard words by the soft intonation of her musical voice. Down the page went the green guide, and presently, forgetting her listener in the beauty of the sad scene, Meg read as if alone, giving a little touch of tragedy to the words of the unhappy queen. If she had seen the brown eyes then, she would have stopped short; but she never looked up, and the lesson was not spoilt for her.

Miss Kate put up her glass, and, having taken a survey of the little tableau before her, shut her sketch-book, saying with condescension.

"You've a nice accent, and, in time, will be a clever reader. I must look after Grace; she is romping"; and Miss Kate strolled away, adding to herself, with a shrug, "I didn't come to chaperone a governess, though she is young and pretty. What odd people these Yankees are!"

"I forgot that English people rather turn up their noses at governesses," said Meg, looking after the retreating figure with an annoyed expression.

"Tutors, also, have rather a hard time of it there, as I know to my sorrow. There's no place like America for us workers, Miss Margaret"; and Mr. Brooke looked so contented and cheerful that Meg was ashamed to lament her hard lot.

"I'm glad I live in it then. I don't like my work, but I get a good deal of satisfaction out of it after all, so I won't complain; I only wish I liked teaching as you do."

"I think you would, if you had Laurie for a pupil. I shall be very sorry to lose him next year," said Mr. Brooke.

"Going to college, I suppose?" Meg's lips asked that question, but her eyes added, "And what becomes of you?"

"Yes; it's high time he went, for he is nearly ready; and as soon as he is off, I shall turn soldier."

"I'm glad of that!" exclaimed Meg; "I should think every young man would want to go; though it is hard for the mothers and sisters who stay at home," she added sorrowfully.

"I have neither, and very few friends, to care whether I live or die," said Mr. Brooke, rather bitterly.

"Laurie and his grandfather would care a great deal, and we should all be very sorry to have any harm happen to you," said Meg heartily.

"Thank you, that sounds pleasant," began Mr. Brooke, looking cheerful again; but, before he could finish his speech, Ned, mounted on the old horse, came lumbering up, to display his equestrian skill before the yound ladies, and there was no more quiet that day.

"Don't you love to ride?" asked Grace of Amy.

"I dote upon it. My sister Meg used to ride, when papa was rich, but we don't keep any horses now, except Ellen Tree," added Amy, laughing.

"Tell me about Ellen Tree; is it a donkey?" asked Grace curiously.

"Why, you see, Jo is crazy about horses, and so am I, but we've only got an old side-saddle, and no horse. Out in the garden is an apple tree that has a nice low branch; so I fix some reins on the part turns up, and we bounce away on Ellen Tree whenever we like."

110

"How funny!" laughed Grace. "I have a pony at home and ride nearly every day in the Park with Fred and Kate; it's very nice, for my friends go too, and the Row is full of ladies and gentlemen."

"Dear, how charming! I hope I shall go abroad some day; but I'd rather go to Rome than the Row," said Amy, who had not the remotest idea what the Row was.

Frank, sitting just behind the little girls, heard what they were saying, and pushed his crutch away from him with an impatient gesture, as he watched the active lads going through all sorts of comical gymnastics. Beth looked up, and said in her shy, yet friendly way, — "I'm afraid you are tired; can I do anything for you?"

"Talk to me, please; it's dull sitting by myself."

"What do you like to talk about?" she asked.

"Well, I like to hear about cricket, and boating, and hunting," said Frank.

"My heart! whatever shall I do! I don't know anything about them," thought Beth; and, forgetting the boy's misfortune in her flurry, she said, hoping to make him talk, "I never saw any hunting, but I suppose you know all about it?"

"I did once; but I'll never hunt again, for I got hurt leaping a confounded five-barred gate; so there's no more horses and hounds for me," said Frank, with a sigh that made Beth hate herself for her innocent blunder.

"Your deer are much prettier than our ugly buffaloes," she said, turning to the prairies for help, and feeling glad that she had read one of boys' books in which Jo delighted.

Buffaloes proved soothing and satisfactory; and, in her eagerness to amuse another, Beth forgot herself, and was quite unconscious of her sister's surprise at the unusual spectacle of Beth talking away to one of the dreadful boys, against whom she begged protection.

"Bless her heart! She pities him, so she is good to him," said Jo, beaming at her from the croquet ground.

An impromptu circus, fox and geese, and an amicable game of croquet finished the afternoon. At sunset the tent was struck, hampers packed, wickets pulled up, boats loaded, and the whole party floated down the river, singing at the tops of their voices. Ned, getting sentimental, warbled a serenade with the pensive refrain —

"Alone, alone, ah! woe, alone,"
and at the lines —

"We each are young, we each have a heart,

Oh, why should we stand thus coldly alone?"
he looked at Meg with such a lackadaisical expression that she laughed outright and spoilt his song.

"How can you be so cruel to me?" he whispered, under cover of a lively chorus; "you've kept close to that starched-up Englishman all day, and now you snub me."

"I didn't mean to; but you looked so funny, I really couldn't help it," replied Meg, passing over the first part of his reproach, for it was quite true that she had shunned him, remembering the Moffat party and the talk after it.

Ned was offended, and turned to Sallie, for consolation, saying to her rather pettishly, "There isn't a bit of flirt in that girl, is there?"

"Not a particle; but she's a dear," returned Sallie, defending her friend.

On the lawn where it had gathered, the little party separated with cordial good-nights and good-byes, for the Vaughans were going to Canada. As the four sisters went home through the garden, Miss Kate looked after them, saying, without the petronising tone in her voice, "In spite of their demonstrative manners, American girls are very nice when one knows them."

"I quite agree with you," said Mr. Brooke.

112

# CASTLES IN THE AIR

Laurie lay luxuriously swinging to and fro in his hammock one warm September afternoon, wondering what his neighbours were about.

"What in the world are those girls about now?" thought Laurie, opening his sleepy eyes. Each wore a large flapping hat, a brown linen pouch slung over one shoulder, and carried a long staff; Meg had a cushion, Jo a book, Beth a dipper, and Amy a portfolio. All walked quietly through the garden, and out at the little back gate, and began to climb the hill that lay between the house and river.

"Well, that's cool!" said Laurie to himself, "to have a picnic and never ask me. They can't be going in the boat, for they haven't got the key. Perhaps they forgot it; I'll take it to them and see what's going on."

Taking the shortest way to the boat-house, he waited for them to appear; but no one came, and he went up the hill to take an observation. A grove of pines covered one part of it, and from the heart of this green spot came a clearer sound than the soft sigh of the pines, or the drowsy chirp of the crickets.

"Here's a landscape!" thought Laurie, peeping through the bushes.

It was rather a pretty picture; for the sisters sat together in the shady nook, with sun and shadow flickering over them — the wind lifting their hair and cooling their cheeks. Meg sat upon her cushion sewing daintily with her white hands, and looking as fresh and sweet as a rose, in her pink dress, among the green. Beth was sorting the cones that lay thick under the hemlock near by, for she made pretty things of them. Amy was sketching a group of ferns, and Jo was

113

knitting as she read aloud. A shadow passed over the boy's face as he watched them, feeling that he ought to go, yet lingering, because home seemed lonely. He stood so still that a squirrel ran down a pine close beside him, saw him suddenly, and skipped back, scolding so shrilly that Beth looked, espied the wistful face behind the birches, and beckoned with a smile.

"May I come in, please? Or shall I be a bother?" he asked, advancing slowly.

Meg lifted her eyebrows, but Jo scowled at her, and said, "Of course you may. We should have asked you before, only we thought you wouldn't care for such a girl's game."

"I always like your games; but if Meg don't want me, I'll go away."

"I've no objection, of you do something; it's against the rule to be idle here," replied Meg.

"Much obliged; I'll do anything if you'll let me stop a bit, for it's as dull as the desert of Sahara down there. Shall I sew, read, cone, draw, or do all at once?"

"Finish this story while I set my heel," said Jo, handing him the book.

"Yes'm," was the meek answer, as he began, doing his best to prove his gratitude for the favour of an admission into the "Busy Bee Society."

The story was not a long one, and, when it was finished, he ventured to ask a few questions.

"Please, mum, could I enquire if this highly instructive institution is a new one?"

"Would you tell him?" asked Meg.

"He'll laugh," said Amy warningly.

"Who cares?" said Jo.

"I guess he'll like it," added Beth.

"Of course I shall! I give you my word I won't laugh. Tell away, Jo, and don't be afraid."

114

"The idea of being afraid of you! Well, you see, we used to play Pilgrim's Progress, and we have been going on with it all winter and summer. Well, we have tried not to waste our holiday, but each has had a task, and worked at it with a will. The vacation is nearly over, the stints are all done, and we are ever so glad that we didn't dawdle."

"Yes, I should think so," and Laurie thought regretfully of his own idle days.

"Mother likes to have us out of doors as much as possible so we bring our work here. We call this hill the 'Delectable Mountain,' for we can look far away and see the country where we hope to live sometime."

Jo pointed, and Laurie sat up to examine; for through an opening in the wood one could look across the wide blue river far over the outskirts of the city, to the green hills that rose to meet the sky.

"Jo talks about the country where we hope to live sometime; the real country, she means, with pigs and chickens and haymaking. It would be nice, but I wish the beautiful country up there was real, and we could ever go to it," said Beth musingly.

"There is a lovelier country even than that, where we shall go, by-and-by, when we are good enough," answered Meg with her sweet voice.

"It seems so long to wait, so hard to do; I want to fly away at once."

"You'll get there Beth, sooner or later, no fear of that," said Jo; "I'm the one that will have to fight and work, and maybe never get in after all."

"You'll have me for company, if that's any comfort. I shall have to do a deal of travelling before I come in sight of your Celestial City. If I arrive late, you'll say a good word for me, won't you, Beth?"

Something in the boy's face troubled his little friend; but she said cheerfully, "If people really want to go, and really try hard all their lives, I think they will get in."

"Wouldn't it be fun if all the castles in the air could come true, and we could live in them!" said Jo.

"I've made such quantities it would be hard to choose which I'd have," said Laurie, lying flat, and throwing cones at the squirrel.

"You'd have to take your favourite one. What is it?" asked Meg.

"After I'd seen as much of the world as I want to, I'd like to settle in Germany, and have as much music as I chose. I'm to be a famous musician myself, and all creation is to rush to hear me; and I'm never to be bothered about money or business, but just enjoy myself, and live for what I like. That's my favourite castle. What's yours, Meg?"

"I should like a lovely house, full of all sorts of luxurious things; nice food, pretty clothes, handsome furniture, and heaps of money. I am to be mistress of it, with plenty of servants, so I never need to work a bit. How I should enjoy it! For I wouldn't be idle, but do good, and make everyone love me dearly."

"Why don't you say you'd have a splendid husband, and some angelic little children? You know your castle wouldn't be perfect without," said blunt Jo.

"You'd have nothing but horses, inkstands, and novels in yours," answered Meg petulantly.

"Wouldn't I though! I'd have a stable full of Arabian steeds, rooms piled with books and I'd write out of a magic inkstand, so that my works should be as famous as Laurie's music. I want to do something splendid before I go into my castle. I think I shall write books, and get rich and famous; that is my favourite dream."

"Mine is to stay at home safe with father and mother, and help take care of the family," said Beth contentedly.

"I have lots of wishes; but the pet one is to be an artist, and go to Rome, and be the best artist in the whole world," was Amy's modest desire.

"We're an ambitious set, aren't we. Every one of us, but Beth, wants to be rich and famous. I wonder if any of us will ever get our wishes," said Laurie, chewing grass.

"I've got the key to my castle in the air; but whether I can unlock the door remains to be seen," observed Jo mysteriously.

"I've got the key to mine, but I'm not allowed to try it. Hang college!" muttered Laurie.

"Here's mine!" and Amy waved her pencil.

"I haven't got any," sait Meg forlornly.

"Yes, you have."

"Where?"

"In your face."

"Nonsense; that's of no use."

Wait and see if it doesn't bring you something worth having," replied the boy, laughing at the thought of a secret which he fancied he knew.

Meg coloured, and looked across the river with the same expectant expression which Mr. Brooke had worn when he told the story of the knight.

"If we are all alive ten years hence, let's meet, and see how many of us have got our wishes," said Jo, always ready with a plan.

"Bless me! How old I shall be — twenty-seven!' exclaimed Meg.

"You and I shall be twenty-six, Teddy; Beth twenty-four, and Amy twenty-two; what a venerable party!" said Jo.

117

"I hope I shall have done something to be proud of by that time; but I'm such a lazy dog, I'm afraid I shall 'dawdle,' Jo."

"You need a motive, mother says; and when you get it, she is sure you'll work splendidly."

"Is she? By Jupiter, I will, if I only get the chance!" cried Laurie, sitting up with sudden energy. "I ought to be satisfied to please grandfather, and I do try, but it's working against the grain and comes hard. He wants me to be an India merchant, as he was, and I'd rather be shot; I hate tea, and silk, and spices, and every sort of rubbish his old ships bring. Going to college ought to satisfy him, for if I give him four years, he ought to let me off from the business; but he's set, and I've got to do just as he did, unless I break away and please myself, as my father did. If there was anyone left to stay with the old gentleman, I'd do it to-morrow!"

"You should do just what your grandfather wishes, my dear boy," said Meg in her most maternal tone. "Do your best at college, and, when he sees that you try to please him, he won't be unjust to you. There is no one else to stay with and love him, and you'd never forgive yourself if you left him without his permission. Don't be dismal, or fret, but do your duty; and you'll get your reward, as good Mr. Brooke has, by being respected and loved."

"What do you know about him?" asked Laurie, grateful for the good advice, but objecting to the lecture.

"Only what your grandpa told mother about him; how he took good care of his mother till she died, and wouldn't go abroad as tutor because he wouldn't leave her; and how he provides now for an old woman who nursed his mother; and never tells anyone, but is as generous and patient and good as he can be."

"So he is, dear old fellow!" said Laurie heartily.

"It's like grandpa to find out all about him, and to tell all his goodness to others. If ever I do get my wish, you'll see what I'll do for Brooke."

"Begin to do something now, by not plaguing his life out," said Meg sharply.

"How do you know I do, miss?"

"I can always tell by his face when he goes away. If you have been good, he looks satisfied, and walks briskly; if you have plagued him, he's sober, and walks slowly."

"Well," I like that! So you keep an account of my good and bad marks in Brooke's face, do you? I see him bow and smile as he passes your window, but I didn't know you'd got a telegraph."

"We haven't; don't be angry, and, oh, don't tell him I said anything! I didn't mean to preach; I only thought Jo was encouraging you in a feeling which you'd be sorry for by-and-by. You are so kind to us, we feel as if you were our brother, and just say what we think; forgive me, I meant kindly!" and Meg offered her hand with a gesture both affectionate and timid.

Ashamed of his momentary pique, Laurie squeezed the kind little hand, and said frankly, "I'm the one to be forgiven."

Bent on showing that he was not offended, he made himself agreeable; wound cotton for Meg, recited poetry to please Jo, shook down cones for Beth, and helped Amy with her ferns — proving himself a fit person to belong to the "Busy Bee Society." In the midst of an animated discussion on the domestic habits of turtles (one of which amiable creatures having strolled up from the river), the faint sound of a bell warned them Hannah had put the tea to "draw," and they would just have time to get home to supper.

"May I come again?" asked Laurie.

"Yes, if you are good," said Meg smiling.

"I'll try."

"Then you may come, and I'll teach you to knit; there's a demand for socks just now," added Jo, waving hers, as they parted at the gate.

That night, when Beth played to Mr. Laurence in the twilight, Laurie, standing in the shadow of the curtain, listened to the little David, whose simple music always quieted his moody spirit, and watched the old man, who sat with his grey head on his hand, thinking tender thoughts of the dead child he had loved so much. Remembering the conversation of the afternoon, the boy said to himself, "I'll let my castle go, and stay with the dear old gentleman while he needs me, for I am all he has."

## CHAPTER FOURTEEN

## SECRETS

Jo was busy up in the garret, for the October days began to grow chilly, and the afternoons were short. For two or three hours the sun lay warmly in at the high window, showing Jo seated on the old sofa writing busily, with her papers spread out upon a trunk before her, while Scrabble, the pet rat, promenaded the beams overhead, accompanied by his oldest son, a fine young fellow, who was evidently proud of his whiskers. Jo scribbled away till the last page was filled, when she signed her name with a flourish, and threw down the pen, exclaiming, — "There, I've done my best! If this doesn't suit, I shall have to wait till I can do better."

Lying back on the sofa, she read the manuscript through making dashes here and there, and putting in many exclamation points, which looked like little balloons; then she tied it with a smart ribbon, and sat looking at it with a sober expression, which showed how earnest her work had been. Jo's desk was an old tin kitchen, which hung against the wall. In it she kept her papers, and a few books, safely shut away from Scrabble. From this tin receptacle Jo produced another manuscript; and, putting both in her pocket, crept quietly downstairs.

She put on her hat and jacket and, going to the back entry window, got out upon the roof at a low porch, swung herself down to the grassy bank, and took a roundabout way to the road. Once there, she hailed a passing omnibus, and rolled away to town.

If anyone had been watching her, he would have thought her movements decidedly peculiar; for, on alighting, she went off at a great pace till she reached a certain number in a busy street. She went into the doorway, looked up the dirty stairs and, after standing still a minute, suddenly dived into the street and walked away as rapidly as she came. This manœuvre she repeated several times, to the amusement of a black-eyed young gentleman lounging in the window of a building opposite. On returning for the third time, Jo gave herself a shake and walked up the stairs looking as if she was going to have all her teeth out.

There was a dentist's sign, among others, which adorned the entrance, and after staring a moment at the pair of artificial jaws which slowly opened and shut, to draw attention to a fine set of teeth, the young gentleman went down to post himself in the opposite doorway, saying.

"It's like her to come alone, but if she has a bad time, she'll need someone to help her home."

In ten minutes Jo came running downstairs with a very red face, and the appearance of a person who had just passed through a trying ordeal. When she saw the young gentleman she looked anything but pleased, and passed him with a nod, but he followed, asking with an air of sympathy, — "Did you have a bad time?"

"Not very."

"You're the oddest fellow I ever saw. How many did you have out?"

Jo looked at her friend as if she did not understand him; then began to laugh.

"There are two which I want to have come out, but I must wait a week."

"What are you laughing at? You are up to some mischief, Jo," said Laurie, looking mystified.

"So are you. What were you doing, sir, up in that billiard saloon?"

"Begging your pardon, ma'am, it wasn't a billiard saloon, but a gymnasium, and I was taking a lesson in fencing."

"I am glad of that."

"Why?"

"You can teach me; and then, when we play *Hamlet*, you can be Laertes, and we'll make a fine thing of the fencing scene."

Laurie burst out with a hearty boy's laugh which made several passers-by smile in spite of themselves.

"I'll teach you whether we play *Hamlet* or not; it's grand fun, and will straighten you up capitally. But I don't believe that was your only reason for saying, 'I'm glad,' in that decided way.

"No; I was glad you were not in the saloon, because I hope you never go to such places. Do you?"

"Not often."

"I wish you wouldn't."

"It's no harm, Jo. I have billiards at home, but it's no fun unless you have good players; so, as I'm fond of it, I come some times and have a game with Ned Moffat or some of the other fellows."

"Oh, dear, I am so sorry, for you'll get to liking it better and better, and will waste time and money, and grow like those dreadful boys. I did hope you'd stay respectable, and be a satisfaction to your friends," said Jo, shaking her head.

"Can't a fellow take a little innocent amusement now and then without losing his respectability?" asked Laurie, looking nettled.

"That depends on how and where he takes it. I don't like Ned and his set, and wish you'd keep out of it. Mother won't let us have him at our house, though he wants to come; and if you grow like him, she won't be willing to have us frolic together as we do now."

"Won't she?" asked Laurie anxiously.

"No, she can't bear fashionable young men, and she'd shut us all up in bandboxes rather than have us associate with them."

"Well, she needn't get out her bandboxes yet; I'm not a fashionable party and don't mean to be; but I do like harmless larks now and then, don't you?"

"Yes; nobody minds them, so lark away, but don't get wild, will you?"

"Are you going to deliver lectures all the way home?" he asked.

"Of course not; why?"

"Because if you are, I'll take a 'bus; if you are not, I'd like to walk with you and tell you something interesting."

"I won't preach any more, and I'd like to hear the news immensely."

"Very well then; come on. It's a secret, and if I tell you, you must tell me yours."

"I haven't got any," began Jo, but stopped suddenly, remembering that she had.

"You know you have; you can't hide anything, so up and 'fess, or I won't tell," cried Laurie.

"Well, I've left two stories with a newspaper man, and he's to give his answer next week," whispered Jo in her confidant's ear.

"Hurrah for Miss March, the celebrated American authoress!" cried Laurie, throwing up his hat and catching it again.

"Where's *your* secret? Play fair, Teddy, or I'll never believe you again."

"I may get into a scrape for telling; but I don't promise not to, so I will, for I never feel easy in my mind till I've told any plummy bit of news I get. I know where Meg's glove is."

"Is that all?" said Jo, looking disappointed.

"It's quite enough for the present, as you'll agree when I tell you where it is."

"Tell, then."

Laurie bent and whispered three words in Jo's ear, which produced a comical change. She stood and stared at him, looking both surprised and displeased, then walked on, saying sharply, "How do you know?"

"Saw it."

"Where?"

"Pocket."

"All this time?"

"Yes; isn't that romantic?"

"No; it's horrid."

"I thought you'd be pleased."

"At the idea of anybody coming to take Meg away? No, thank you."

"You'll feel better about it when somebody comes to take you away."

"I'd like to see anyone try it," cried Jo fiercely.

"So should I!" and Laurie chuckled at the idea.

"I don't think secrets agree with me; I feel rumpled up in my mind since you told me that," said Jo, rather ungratefully.

"Race down this hill with me, and you'll be al right," suggested Laurie.

No one was in sight; the smooth road sloped invitingly before her, and finding the temptation irresistible, Jo darted away, soon leaving hat and comb behind her, and scattering hair-pins as she ran. Laurie reached the goal firt, and was quite satisfied with the success of his treatment; for his Atalanta came panting up with flying hair, bright eyes, ruddy cheeks, and no signs of dissatisfaction in her face.

"I wish I was a horse; then I could run for miles in this splendid air, and not lose my breath. Go, pick up my things, like a cherub as you are," said Jo, dropping down under a maple-tree.

Laurie leisurely departed to recover the lost property, and Jo bundled up her braids, hoping no one would pass by till she was tidy again. But someone did pass, and who should it be but Meg, looking particularly lady-like in her state and festive suit, for she had been making calls.

"What in the world are you doing here?" she asked, regarding her dishevelled sister with well-bred surprise.

"Getting leaves," meekly answered Jo sorting the rosy handful she had just swept up.

"And hair-pins," added Laurie, throwing half a dozen into Jo's lap. "They grow on this road, Meg; so do combs and brown straw hats."

"You have been running, Jo; how could you? When *will* you stop such romping ways?" said Meg reprovingly.

"Never till I'm stiff and old, and have to use a crutch. Don't try to make me grow up before my time, Meg; it's hard enough to have you change all of a sudden; let me be a little girl as long as I can."

As she spoke, Jo bent over her work to hide the trembling of her lips; for lately she had felt that Margaret was fast getting to be a woman, and Laurie's secret made her dread the separation which must surely come some time, and now seemed very near. He saw the trouble in her face, and drew Meg's attention from it by asking quickly, "Where have you been calling, all so fine?"

"At the Gardiners'; and Sallie has been telling me all about Belle Moffat's wedding. It was very splendid, and they have gone to spend the winter in Paris; just think how delightful that must be!"

"Do you envy her, Meg?" said Laurie.

"I'm afraid I do."

"I'm glad of it!" muttered Jo, tying on her hat with a jerk.

"Why?" asked Meg, looking surprised.

"Because, if you care much about riches, you will never go and marry a poor man," said Jo.

"I shall never 'go and marry' anyone," observed Meg, walking on with great dignity, while the others followed, laughing, whispering, skipping stones, and "behaving like children," as Meg said to herself, though she might have been tempted to join them if she had not her best dress on.

For a week or two Jo behaved so queerly that her sisters got quite bewildered. She rushed to the door when the postman rang; was rude to Mr. Brooke whenever they met; would sit looking at Meg, with a woebegone face, occasionally jumping up to shake, and then to kiss her; Laurie and she were always making signs to one another, till the girls declared they had both lost their wits. On the second Saturday after Jo got out of the window, Meg, as she sat sewing at her window was scandalised by the sight of Laurie chasing Jo all over the garden, and finally capturing her in Amy's bower. What went on there Meg could not see, but shrieks of laughter were heard, followed by the murmur of voices, and a great flapping of newspapers.

"What shall we do with that girl? She never *will* behave like a young lady," sighed Meg.

In a few minutes Jo bounced in, laid herself on the sofa, and affected to read.

"Have you anything interesting there?" asked Meg.

"Nothing but a story! don't amount to much, I guess," returned Jo.

"You'd better read it aloud; that will amuse us, and keep you out of mischief," said Amy.

"What's the name?" asked Beth.

*"The Rival Painters."*

"That sounds well; read it," said Meg.

With a loud "hem!" Jo began to read very fast. The girls listened with interest, for the tale was romantic, and somewhat pathetic, as most of the caracters died in the end.

"I like that about the splendid picture," was Amy's approving remark, as Jo paused.

"I prefer the lovering part. Viola and Angelo are two of our favourite names; isn't that queer?" said Meg.

"Who wrote it?" asked Beth, who had caught a glimpse of Jo's face.

The reader suddenly sat up, cast away the paper displaying a flushed countenance, and, with a funny mixture of solemnity and excitement, replied in a loud voice, "Your sister!"

"You?" cried Meg, dropping her work.

"It's very good," said Amy critically.

"I knew it! Oh, my Jo, I *am* so proud!" and Beth ran to hug her sister.

Dear me, how delighted they all were; how Meg wouldn't believe it till she saw the words "Miss Josephine March," actually printed in the paper; how graciously Amy criticised the artistic parts of the story, and offered hints for a sequel which unfortunately couldn't be carried out, as the hero and heroine were dead; how Beth got excited and skipped and sung for joy; how Hannah came in to exclaim, "Sakes alive! well, I never!" in great astonishment at "that Jo's doings"; how proud Mrs. March was when she knew it; how Jo laughed, with tears in her eyes, as she declared she might well be a peacock and done with it.

"Tell us about it." "When did it come?" "How much did you get for it?" "What will Father say?" "Won't Laurie laugh!" cried all the family, all in one breath, as they clung about Jo.

"Stop jabbering, girls, and I'll tell you everything," said Jo. Having told how she disposed of her tales, Jo added, — "And when I went to get my answer, the man said he liked them both, but didn't pay beginners, only let them print in his paper, and noticed the stories. It was good practice, he said, and when the beginners improved any, one would pay. So I let him have the two stories, and today this was sent to me, and Laurie caught me with it, and insisted on seeing it, so I let him; and he said it was good, and I shall write more, and he's going to get the next paid for; and, oh! — I *am* so happy, for in time I may be able to support myself and help the girls."

Jo's breath gave out here; and, wrapping her head in the paper, she bedewed her little story with a few natural tears; for to be independent, and earn the praise of those she loved were the dearest wishes of her heart, and this seemed to be the first step towards that happy end.

## CHAPTER FIFTEEN

## A TELEGRAM

"November is the most disagreeable month in the whole year," said Margaret, standing at the window one dull afternoon, looking out at the frost-bitten garden.

"That's the reason I was born in it," observed Jo pensively.

"If something very pleasant should happen now, we should think it a delightful month," said Beth.

Jo groaned and leaned both elbows on the table in a despondent attitude; but Amy spatted away energetically; and Beth who sat at the other window, said smiling, "Two pleasant things are going to happen right away: Marmee is coming down the street, and Laurie is tramping through the garden as if he had something nice to tell."

In they both came, Mrs. March with her usual question, "Any letter from father, girls?" and Laurie to say, "Won't some of you come for a drive? I've been pegging away at mathematics till my head is in a muddle. It's a dull day, but the air isn't bad, and I'm going to take Brooke home, so it will be gay inside, if it isn't out. Come, Jo, you and Beth will go, won't you?"

"Of course we will."

"Much obliged, but I'm busy"; and Meg whisked out her work-basket for she had agreed with her mother that it was best, for her at least, not to drive often with the young gentleman.

"Can I do anything for you, Madam Mother?" asked Laurie, leaning over Mrs. March's chair, with the affectionate look and tone he always gave her.

"No, thank you, except call at the office, if you'll be so kind, dear. It's our day for a letter, and the postman hasn't been. Father is as regular as the sun, but there's some delay on the way, perhaps."

A sharp ring interrupted her, and a minute after Hannah came in.

"It's one of them horrid telegraph things, mum," she said, handling it as if she were afraid it would explode.

At the word "telegraph," Mrs. March snatched it, read the two lines it contained, and dropped back into her chair as white as if the little paper had sent a bullet to her heart. Laurie dashed downstairs for water, while Meg and Hannah supported her, and Jo read aloud in a frightened voice, —

"MRS MARCH : —

"Your husband is very ill. Come at once."

Mrs. March was herself again directly: read the message over, and stretched out her arms to her daughters, saying, "I shall go at once, but it may be too late; oh, children, children; help me to bear it!"

For several minutes there was nothing but the sound of sobbing in the room, mingled with broken words of comfort, tender assurances of help, and hopeful whispers that died away in tears. Poor Hannah was the first to recover, and with unconscious wisdom she set all the rest a good example.

"The Lord keep the dear man ! I won't waste no time a-cryin', but get things ready right away, mum," she said heartily, as she wiped her face on her apron, gave her mistress a warm shake of the hand with her own hard one, and went away to work like three women in one.

"She's right; there's no time for tears now. Be calm girls, and let me think."

They tried to be calm, poor things, as their mother sat up, looking pale, but steady, and put away her grief to think and plan for them.

"Where's Laurie?" she asked presently, when she had collected her thoughts.

"Here, ma'am; oh, let me do something!" cried the boy, hurrying from the next room, whither he had withdrawn.

"Send a telegram saying I will come at once. The next train goes early in the morning."

"What else? The horses are ready; I can go anywhere, — do anything," he said, looking ready to fly to the ends of the earth.

"Leave a note at Aunt March's. Jo, give me that pen and paper."

Tearing off the blank side of one of her newly-copied pages, Jo drew the table before her mother, well knowing that money for the long, sad journey must be borrowed, and feeling as if she could do anything to add a little to the sum for her father.

"Now go, dear; but don't kill yourself driving at a desperate pace; there is no need for that."

Mrs. March's warming was evidently thrown away; for five minutes later Laurie tore by the window, on his own fleet horse, riding as for life.

"Jo, run to the rooms and tell Mrs. King that I can't come. On the way get these things. I'll put them down; they'll be needed and I must go prepared for nursing. Hospital stores are not always good. Beth, go and ask. Mr. Laurence for a couple of bottles of old wine. I'm not too proud to beg for father. Amy, tell Hannah to get down the black trunk; and, Meg, come and help me find my things, for I'm half bewildered."

131

Writing, thinking, and directing all at once might well bewilder the poor lady, and Meg begged her to sit quietly in her room for a little while, and let them work. Everyone scattered, like leaves before a gust of wind; and the quiet, happy household was broken up.

Mr. Laurence came hurrying back with Beth, bringing every comfort the kind old gentleman could think of for the invalid, and friendliest promises of protection for the girls during their mother's absence. There was nothing he didn't offer, from his own dressing-gown to himself as escort. But that last was impossible. Mrs. March would not hear of the old gentleman's undertaking the long journey; yet an expression of relief was visible when he spoke of it, for anxiety ill fits one for travelling. He saw the look, knit his eyebrows, rubbed his hands, and marched abruptly away, saying he'd be back directly. No one had time to think of him again till, as Meg ran through the entry, with a pair of rubbers in one hand and a cup of tea in the other, she came suddenly upon Mr. Brooke.

"I'm very sorry to hear of this, Miss March," he said, in the kind, quiet voice which sounded very pleasantly to her perturbed spirit. "I came to offer myself as escort to your mother."

Down dropped the rubbers, and the tea was very near following, as Meg put out her hand, with a face full of gratitude, that Mr. Brooke would have felt repaid for a much greater sacrifice.

"How kind you all are! Mother will accept, I'm sure; and it will be such a relief to know that she had someone to take care of her. Thank you very, very much!"

Meg spoke earnestly, and forgot herself entirely till something in the brown eyes looking down at her made her remember the cooling tea, and lead the way into the parlour

132

Everything was arranged by the time Laurie returned with a note from Aunt March, enclosing the desired sum, and a few lines repeating that she had always told them it was absurd for March to go into the army, always predicted that no good would come of it, and hoped they would take her advice next time. Mrs. March put the not in the fire, the money in her purse, and went on with her preparations, with her lips folded tightly.

The short afternoon wore away; all the other errands were done, and Meg and her mother busy at some necessary needlework, while Beth and Amy got tea, and Hannah finished her ironing, with what she called a "slap and a bang," but still Jo did not come. They began to get anxious; and Laurie went off to find her. He missed her, however, and she came walking in with a very queer expression of countenance, which puzzled the family as did the roll of bills she laid before her mother, saying, with a little choke in her voice, "That's my contribution towards making father comfortable, and bringing him home!"

"My dear, where did you get it? Twenty-five dollars! I hope you haven't done anything rash?"

"No, it's mine honestly; I didn't beg, borrow, or steal it. I earned it; and I don't think you'll blame me, for I only sold what was my own."

As she spoke, Jo took off her bonnet, and a general outcry arose, for all her abundant hais was cut short.

"Your hair! Your beautiful hair!" "Oh, Jo, how could you? Your one beauty." "She don't look like my Jo any more, but I love her dearly for it!"

As everyone exclaimed, and Beth hugged the cropped head tenderly, Jo assumed an indifferent air, which did not deceive anyone a particle, and said, rumpling up the brown bush, "It doesn't affect the fate of the nation, so don't wail, Beth. It will do my brains good to have that mop taken off; and the barber said I could soon have a curly crop, which will be boyish, becoming, and easy to keep in order."

"What made you do it?" asked Amy, who would have as soon thought of cutting off her head as her pretty hair.

"Well, I was wild to do something for father," replied Jo, as they gathered about the table. "Meg gave all her quarterly salary towards the rent, and I only got some clothes with mine, so I felt wicked, and was bound to have some money, if I sold the nose off my face to get it."

"You needn't feel wicked, my child; you had no winter things, and got the simplest, with your own hard earnings," said Mrs. March, with a look that warmed Jo's heart.

"I hadn't the least idea of selling my hair at first, but as I went along I kept thinking *what* I could do, in a barber's window I saw tails of hair with the prices marked; and one black tail, longer, but no so thick as mine, was forty dollars. It came over me all of a sudden that I had one thing to make money out of, and walked in, asked if they bought hair, and what they would give for mine."

"I don't see how you dared to do it," said Beth, in a tone of awe.

"Oh, he was a little man, who rather stared at first as if he wasn't used to having girls bounce into his shop and ask him to buy their hair. He said he didn't care about mine; it wasn't the fashionable colour, and he never paid much for it in the first place; the work put into it made it dear, and so on. It was getting late, and I was afraid, if it wasn't done right away, that I shouldn't have it done at all; so I begged him to take it, and told him why I was in such a hurry. It was silly, I dare say, but it changed his mind, for I got rather excited, and told the story in my topsy-turvy way, and his wife heard, and said so kindly, —

134

" 'Take it, Thomas, and oblige the young lady; I'd do as much for our Jimmy any day if I had a spire of hair worth selling.' "

"Who was Jimmy?" asked Amy, who liked to have things explained as they went along.

"Her son, she said, who is in the army. She talked away all the time the man clipped, and diverted my mind nicely."

"Didn't you feel dreadfully when the first cut came?" asked Meg, with a shiver.

"I took a last look at my hair while the man got his things, and that was the end of it. I will confess, though, I felt queer when I saw the dear old hair laid out on the table. It almost seemed as if I'd had an arm or leg off. The woman saw me look at it, and picked out a long lock for me to keep. I'll give it to you, Marmee, just to remember past glories by."

Mrs. March folded the wavy, chestnut lock, and laid it away with a short grey one in her desk.

No one wanted to go to bed when, at ten o'clock, Mrs. March put the last finished job by, and said, "Come, girls." Beth went to the piano and played their father's favourite hymn; all began bravely, but broke down one by one till Beth was left alone, singing with all her heart.

"Go to bed, and don't talk, for we must be up early, and shall need all the sleep we can get. Good-night, my darlings," said Mrs. March, as the hymn ended.

They kissed her quietly, and went to bed as silently as if the dear invalid lay in the next room. Beth and Amy soon fell asleep in spite of the great trouble, but Meg lay awake, thinking the most serious thoughts she had ever known in her short life. Jo lay motionless, and her sister fancied that she was asleep, till a stifled sob made her exclaim, as she touched a wet cheek, —

"Jo, dear, what is it? Are you crying about father?"

"No, not now."

"What then?"

"My — my hair," burst out poor Jo, trying vainly to smother her emotion in the pillow.

It did not sound at all comical to Meg, who kissed and caressed the afflicted heroine in the tenderest manner.

"I'm not sorry," protested Jo, with a choke. "I'd do it again tomorrow, if I could. It's only the vain, selfish part of me that goes and cries in this silly way. Don't tell anyone; it's all over now. I thought you were asleep. How came you to be awake?"

"I can't sleep; I'm so anxious," said Meg.

"Think of something pleasant, and you'll soon drop off."

"I tried it, but felt wider awake that ever."

"What did you think of?"

"Handsome faces; eyes particularly," answered Meg smilingly, to herself in the dark.

"What colour do you like best?"

"Brown — that is, sometimes — blue are lovely."

Jo laughed, and Meg sharply ordered her not to talk, then amiably promised to make her hair curl, and fell asleep to dream of living in her castle in the air.

The clocks were striking midnight, as a figure glided quietly from bed to bed, smoothing a coverlet here, setting a pillow there, and pausing to look long and tenderly at each unconscious face. As she lifted the curtain to look out into the dreary night, the moon broke suddenly from behind the clouds, and shone upon her like a bright face, which seemed to whisper. "Be comforted, dear soul! there is light behind the clouds."

## CHAPTER SIXTEEN

# BETTER NEWS

In the cold grey dawn the sisters lit their lamp and read their chapter with an earnestness never felt before. Everything seemed strange when they went down: so dim and still outside, so full of life and bustle within. Breakfast at that early hour seemed odd, and even Hannah's familiar face looked unnatural as she flew about her kitchen with her nightcap on. The big trunk stood ready in the hall, mother's cloak and bonnet lay on the sofa, and mother herself sat trying to eat, but looking pale and worn with sleeplessness and anxiety. Meg's eyes kept filling in spite of herself; Jo was obliged to hide her face in the kitchen roller more than once; and the little girls' young faces wore a grave, troubled expression, as if sorrow was a new experience to them.

Nobody talked much, but, as the time drew near, and they sat waiting for the carriage, Mrs. March said to the girls, "Children, I leave you to Hannah's care and Mr. Laurence's protection. Don't grieve and fret when I am gone. Go on with your work as usual, for work is a blessed solace. Hope, and keep busy; and, whatever happens, remember that you can never be fatherless."

"Yes, mother."

"Meg, dear, be prudent, watch over your sisters; consult Hannah, and, in any perplexity, go to Mr. Laurence. Be patient, Jo; don't get despondent, or do rash things; write to me often, and be faithful to the little home duties; and you, Amy, help all you can, be obedient, and keep happy."

"We will, mother! we will!"

The rattle of an approaching carriage made them all start. That was the hard minute, but the girls stood it well; no one cried or uttered a lamentation, though their hearts were heavy as they sent loving messages to father, remembering that it might be too late to deliver them. They kissed their mother quietly, and tried to wave their hands cheerfully when she drove away.

Laurie and his grandfather came over to see her off, and Mr. Brooke looked so strong, and sensible, and kind, that the girls christened him "Mr. Greatheart," on the spot.

"Good-bye, my darlings! God bless and keep us all," whispered Mrs. March, as she kissed one dear little face after the other, and hurried into the carriage.

As she rolled away, the sun came out, and, looking back she saw it shining on the group at the gate, like a good omen. They saw it also, and smiled and waved their hands; and the last thing she beheld, as she turned the corner, was the four bright faces, and behind them, like a body-guard, old Mr. Laurence, faithful Hannah, and devoted Laurie.

"I feel as if there had been an earthquake," said Jo, as their neighbours went home to breakfast.

Beth opened her lips to say something, but could only point to the pile of nicely-mended hose which lay on mother's table, showing that in her last hurried moments she had thought and worked for them. It was a little thing, but it went straight to their hearts; and in spite of brave resolutions, they all broke down, and cried bitterly.

Hannah wisely allowed them to relieve their feelings; and when the shower showed signs of clearing up, she came to the rescue, armed with a coffee-pot.

"Now, my dear young ladies, remember what your ma said, and don't fret; come and have a cup of coffee all round, and then let's fall to work."

Coffee was a treat, and Hannah showed great tact in making it that morning. They drew up to the table, exchanged their handkerchiefs for napkins, and, in ten minutes, were all right again.

" 'Hope and keep busy;' that's the motto for us, so let's see who will remember it best. I shall go to Aunt March, as usual; oh, won't she lecture, though!" said Jo.

"I shall go to my Kings, though I'd much rather stay at home and attend to things here," said Meg.

"No need of that; Beth and I can keep house perfectly well," put in Amy, with an important air. "Hannah will tell us what to do; and we'll have everything nice when you come home," added Beth, getting out her mop and dish-tub without delay.

"I think anxiety is very interesting," observed Amy, eating sugar pensively.

The girls couldn't help laughing, and felt better for it, though Meg shook her head at the young lady who could find consolation in a sugar-bowl.

The sight of the turnovers made Jo sober again; and, when the two went out to their daily tasks, they looked sorrowfully back at the window where they were accustomed to see mother's face. It was gone; but Beth had remembered the little household ceremony, and there she was, nodding away at them like a rosy-faced mandarin.

"That's so like my Beth!" said Jo, waving her hat, with a grateful face. "Good-bye, Meggy; I hope the Kings won't train today. Don't fret about father, dear," she added, as they parted.

"And I hope Aunt March won't croak. Your hair is becoming, and it looks very boyish and nice," returned Meg, trying not to smile at the curly head, which looked comically small on her sister's shoulders.

"That's my only comfort"; and, touching her hat à la Laurie, away went Jo, feeling like a shorn sheep on a wintry day.

News from their father comforted the girls; for, though dangerously ill, the presence of the tenderest of nurses had already done him good. Mr. Brooke sent a bulletin every day, and, as the head of the family, Meg insisted on reading the despatches, which grew more cheering as the week passed.

Everyone was eager to write, and plump envelopes were carefully poked into the letter-box, by one or other of the sisters, who felt rather important with their Washington correspondence.

## CHAPTER SEVENTEEN

# LITTLE FAITHFUL

For a week the amount of virtue in the old house would have supplied the neighbourhood. It was amazing, for everyone seemed in a heavenly frame of mind, and self-denial was all the fashion. Relieved of their first anxiety about their father, the girls insensibly relaxed their praiseworthy efforts a little and began to fall back into the old ways.

Jo caught a bad cold through neglecting to cover the shorn head enough, and was ordered to stay at home till she was better. Jo liked this, and subsided on to the sofa to nurse the cold with arsenicum and books. Amy found that housework and art did not go well together, and returned to her mud pies. Meg went daily to her kingdom, and sewed at home, but much time was spent in writing long letters to her mother, or reading the Washington despatches over and over. Beth kept on with only slight relapses into idleness or grieving. All the little duties were faithfully done each day, and many of her sisters' also, for they were forgetful, and the house seemed like a clock whose pendulum was gone a-visiting. When her heart got heavy with longings for mother, or fears for father, she went away into a certain closet, hid her face in the folds

140

of a certain dear old gown, and made her little moan, and prayed her little prayer quietly by herself. Nobody knew what cheered her up after a sober fit, but everyone felt how sweet and helpful Beth was, and fell into a way of going to her for comfort or advice in their small affairs.

All were unconscious that this experience was a test of character; and when the first excitement was over, felt that they had done well, and deserved praise. So they did; but their mistake was in ceasing to do well.

"Meg, I wish you'd go and see the Hummels; you know mother told us not to forget them," said Beth, ten days after Mrs. March's departure.

"I'm too tired to go this afternoon," replied Meg, rocking comfortably as she sewed.

"Can't you, Jo?" asked Beth.

"Too stormy for me, with my cold."

"I thought it was most well."

"It's well enough to go out with Laurie, but not well enough to go to the Hummels," said Jo, laughing, but looking a little ashamed.

"Why don't you go yourself?" asked Meg.

"I *have* been every day, but the baby is sick, and I don't know what to do for it. Mrs. Hummel goes away to work, and Lottchen takes care of it; but it gets sicker and sicker, and I think you or Hannah ought to go."

Beth spoke earnestly, and Meg promised she would go tomorrow.

"Ask Hannah for some nice little mess, and take it round, Beth; the air will do you good," said Jo, adding apologetically, "I'd go, but I want to finish my story."

"My head aches, and I'm tired, so I thought maybe some of you would go," said Beth.

"Amy will be in presently, and she will run down for us," suggested Meg.

So Beth lay down on the sofa, the others returned to their work, and the Hummels were forgotten. An hour passed, Amy did not come; Meg went to her room to try on a new dress; Jo was absorbed in her story, and Hannah was sound asleep before the kitchen fire, when Beth quietly put on her hood, filled the basket with odds and ends for the poor children, and went out into the chilly air with a heavy head, and a grieved look in her patient eyes. It was late when she came back, and no one saw her creep upstairs and shut herself in her mother's room. Half an hour after Jo went to "mother's closet" for something, and there found Beth sitting on the medicine chest looking very grave, with red eyes, and a camphor bottle in her hand.

"Christopher Columbus! what's the matter?" cried Jo, as Beth put out her hand as if to warn her off, and asked quickly, — "You've had scarlet fever, haven't you?"

"Years ago, when Meg did. Why?"

"Then I'll tell you — oh, Jo, the baby's dead!"

"What baby?"

"Mrs. Hummel's; it died in my lap before she got home," cried Beth, with a sob.

"My poor dear, how dreadful for you. I ought to have gone," said Jo, taking her sister in her lap as she sat down in her mother's big chair, with a remorseful face.

"It wasn't dreadful, Jo, only so sad! I saw in a minute that it was sicker, but Lottchen said her mother had gone for a doctor, so I took baby and let Lotty rest. It seemed asleep, but all of a sudden it gave a little cry, and trembled, and then lay very still. I tried to warm its feet, and Lotty gave it some milk, but it didn't stir, and I knew it was dead."

"Don't cry, dear! what did you do?"

"I just sat and held it softly till Mrs. Hummel came with the doctor. He said it was dead, and looked at Heinrich and Minna, who have got sore throats. 'Scarlet fever, ma'am;

142

ought to have called me before,' he said crossly. Mrs. Hummel told him she was poor, and had tried to cure the baby herself. He smilled then, and was kinder, but it was very sad, and I cried with them, till he turned, all of a sudden, and told me to go home and take belladonna right away, or I'd have the fever."

"No, you won't!" cried Jo, hugging her close, with a frightened look. "Oh; Beth, if you should be sick I never could forgive myself!"

"Don't be frightened, I guess I shan't have it badly; I looked in mother's book, and saw it begins with headache, sore throat, and queer feelings like mine, so I did take some belladonna, and I feel better," said Beth, laying her cold hands on her hot forehead, and trying to look well.

"If mother was only at home!" exclaimed Jo, seizing the book. She read a page, looked at Beth, felt her head, peeped into her throat, and then said gravely, "I'm afraid you're going to have it, Beth. I'll call Hannah; she knows all about sickness."

"Don't let Amy come; she never had it, and I should hate to give it to her. Can't you and Meg have it over again?" asked Beth anxiously.

"I guess not; don't care if I do; serve me right, selfish pig, to let you go, and stay writing rubbish myself!" muttered Jo, as she went to consult Hannah.

The good soul was wide awake in a minute, and took the lead at once, assuring Jo that there was no need to worry; everyone had scarlet fever, and if rightly treated nobody died; all of which Jo believed, and felt much relieved as they went up to call Meg.

"Now I'll tell you what we'll do," said Hannah, when she had exclaimed and questioned Beth; "we will have Dr. Bangs, just to look at you, dear; then we'll send Amy off to Aunt

March's for a spell to keep her out of harm's way, and one of you girls can stay at home and amuse Beth for a day or two."

"I shall stay, of course; I'm the oldest," began Meg, looking anxious and self-reproachful.

"I shall, because it's my fault she is sick; I told mother I'd do the errands, and I haven't," said Jo decidedly.

"Which will you have, Beth? there ain't no need of but one," said Hannah.

"Jo, please"; and Beth leaned her head against her sister with a contented look, which settled the point.

"I'll go and tell Amy," said Meg, feeling a little hurt, yet rather relieved on the whole, for she did not like nursing, and Jo did.

Amy rebelled outright, and declared that she had rather have the fever than go to Aunt March. Meg left in despair, to ask Hannah what should be done. Before she came back, Laurie walked into the parlour, to find Amy sobbing, with her head in the sofa cushions. She told her story, expecting to be consoled; but Laurie only put his hands in his pockets and walked about the room, whistling softly. Presently, he sat down beside her, and said, in his most wheedlesome tone, "Now be a sensible little woman, and hear what a jolly plan I've got. You go to Aunt March's and I'll come and take you out every day, driving or walking, and we'll have capital times."

"But it's dull at Aunt March's, and she is so cross," said Amy, looking rather frightened.

"It won't be dull with me popping in every day to tell how Beth is, and take you out gallivanting."

"Will you take me out in the trotting wagon with Puck?"

"On my honour as a gentleman."

"And come every single day?"

"See if I don't."

"And bring me back the minute Beth is well?"

"The identical minute."

"And go to the theatre truly?"

"Well — I guess — I will," said Amy slowly.

"Good girl! Sing out for Meg, and tell her you'll give in," said Laurie.

Meg and Jo came running down to behold the miracle which had been wrought; and Amy, feeling very precious and self-sacrificing promised to go.

"How is the little dear?" asked Laurie; for Beth was his special pet.

"She is lying down on mother's bed, and feels better. The baby's death troubled her, but I dare say she has only got cold. Hannah *says* she thinks so; but she *looks* worried, and that makes me fidgety," answered Meg.

"What a trying world it is!" said Jo, rumpling up her hair in a fretful way. "No sooner do we get out of one trouble than down comes another."

"Well, don't make a porcupine of yourself; it isn't becoming. Settle your wig, Jo, and tell me if I shall telegraph to your mother, or do anything?" asked Laurie.

"That is what troubles me," said Meg. "I think we ought to tell her if Beth is really ill, but Hannah says we mustn't, for mother can't leave father, and it will only make them anxious. Beth won't be sick long, and Hannah knows just what to do."

"Hum, well, I can't say. Suppose you ask grandfather, after the doctor has been?"

"We will; Jo, go and get Dr. Bangs at once," commanded Meg; "we can't decide anything till he has been."

"Stay where you are, Jo; I'm errand boy to this establishment," said Laurie, taking up his cap.

Dr. Bangs came, said Beth had symptoms of the fever, but thought she would have it lightly, though he had looked sober over the Hummel story. Amy was ordered off at once, and provided with something to ward off danger; she departed in a great state, with Jo and Laurie as escort.

Aunt March received them with her usual hospitality.

"What do you want now?" she asked, looking sharply over her spectacles, while the parrot sitting on the back of her chair called out, — "Go away; no boys allowed here."

Laurie retired to the window, and Jo told her story.

"No more than I expected, if you are allowed to go poking about among poor folks. Amy can stay and make herself useful if she isn't sick, which I've no doubt she will be, — looks like it now. Don't cry; it worries me to hear people sniff."

Amy was on the point of crying, but Laurie slyly pulled the parrot's tail which caused Polly to utter an astonished croak, and call out, — "Bless my boots!" in such a funny way that she laughed instead.

"What do you hear from your mother?" asked the old lady gruffly.

"Father is much better," replied Jo, trying to keep sober.

"Oh, is he? Well, that won't last long, I fancy; March never had any stamina," was the cheerful reply.

"Ha, ha! never say die, take a pinch of snuff, good-bye, good-bye!" squalled Polly, dancing on her perch and clawing at the old lady's cap.

"Hold your tongue, you disrespectful old bird! and, Jo, you'd better go at once; it isn't proper to be gadding about so late with a rattle-pated boy like —"

"Hold your tongue, you disrespectful old bird!" cried Polly, tumbling off the chair with a bounce and running to peck the "rattle-pated" boy, who was shaking with laughter at the last speech.

146

"I don't think I *can* bear it, but I'll try," thought Amy, as she was left alone with Aunt March.

"Get along, you're a fright!" screamed Polly; and at that rude speech Amy could not restrain a sniff.

## CHAPTER EIGHTEEN

# DARK DAYS

Beth did have the fever, and was much sicker than anyone but Hannah and the doctor suspected. The girls knew nothing about illness, and Mr. Laurence was not allowed to see her, so Hannah had everything her own way, and Dr. Bangs did his best, but left a good deal to the excellent nurse. Meg stayed at home, lest she should infect the Kings, and kept house feeling very anxious, and a little guilty, when she wrote letters in which no mention was made of Beth's illness. She could not think it right to deceive her mother, but Hannah wouldn't hear of "Mrs. March being told and worried just for a trifle." Jo devoted herself to Beth day and night; not a hard task, for Beth was very patient, and bore her pain uncomplainingly. But there came a time when during the fever fits she began to talk in a hoarse, broken voice, to play on the coverlet, as if on her beloved little piano, and try to sing with a throat so swollen that there was no music left; a time when she did not know the familiar faces round her, but addressed them by wrong names, and called imploringly for her mother. Then Jo grew frightened, Meg begged to be allowed to write the truth, and even Hannah said she "would think of it, though there was no danger *yet*." A letter from Washington added to their trouble, for Mr. March had had a relapse, and could not think of coming home for a long while.

How dark the days seemed now, and how heavy were the hearts of the sisters as they worked and waited, while the shadow of death hovered over the once happy home! Then it was that Margaret, sitting alone, with tears dropping often on her work, felt how rich she had been in things more precious that any luxuries money could buy. Then it was that Jo, living in the darkened room with that suffering little sister learned to see the beauty of Beth's nature, to feel how deep a place she filled in all hearts, and to acknowledge the worth of Beth's unselfish ambition; to live for others, and make home happy by the exercise of those simple virtues which all may possess, and which all should value more than talent, wealth or beauty. And Amy, in her exile, longed eagerly to be at home, that she might work for Beth, feeling now that no service would be irksome. Laurie haunted the house like a restless ghost, and Mr. Laurence locked the grand piano, because he could not bear to be reminded of the young neighbour who used to make the twilight pleasant for him. Everyone missed Beth. The milkman, baker, grocer, and butcher inquired how she did; poor Mrs. Hummel came to beg pardon for her thoughtlessness, and to get a shroud for Minna; the neighbours sent all sorts of comforts and good wishes, and even those who knew her best were surprised to find how many friends shy little Beth had made.

Meanwhile, she lay on her bed with old Joanna at her side, for even in her wanderings she did not forget the forlorn protegee. In her quiet hours, she was full of anxiety about Jo. She sent loving messages to Amy, bade them tell her mother that she would write soon; and often begged for pencil and paper to try to say a word, that father might not think she had neglected him. But soon even these intervals of consciousness ended, and she lay hour after hour tossing to and fro with incoherent words on her lips, or sank into a heavy sleep which brought her no refreshment. Dr. Bangs

148

came twice a day. Hannah sat up at night, Meg kept a telegram in her desk all ready to send off at any minute, and Jo never stirred from Beth's side.

The first of December was a wintry day indeed to them, for a bitter wind blew, snow fell fast, and the year seemed getting ready for its death. When Dr. Bangs came that morning, he looked long at Beth, held the hot hand in both his own a minute, and laid it gently down, saying, in a low tone, to Hannah, — "If Mrs. March *can* leave her husband, she'd better be sent for."

Hannah nodded without speaking, for her lips twitched nervously; Meg dropped down into a chair, the strength seemed to go out of her limbs at the sound of those words, and Jo, after standing with a pale face for a minute, ran to the parlour, snatched up the telegram, and, throwing on her things, rushed out into the storm. She was soon back, and, while noiselessly taking off her cloak, Laurie came in with a letter, saying that Mr. March was mending again. Jo read it thankfully, but her heavy weight did not seem lifted off her heart, and her face was so full of misery that Laurie asked quickly, — "What is it? is Beth worse?"

"I've sent for mother," said Jo, tugging at her rubber boots with a tragical expression.

"Good for you, Jo! Did you do it on your own responsibility?" asked Laurie, as he seated her in the hall chair, and took off the rebellious boots, seeing how her hands shook.

"No, the doctor told us to."

"Oh, Jo! it's not so bad as that?" cried Laurie.

"Yes, it is; she don't know us; she don't look like my Beth, and there's nobody to help us bear it; mother and father both gone, and God seems so far away I can't find Him."

As the tears streamed fast down poor Jo's cheeks, she stretched out her hand, as if groping in the dark and Laurie took it in his, whispering, with a lump in his throat, — "I'm here; hold on to me, Jo, dear!"

She could not speak, but she did "hold on" and the warm grasp of the friendly human hand comforted her sore heart. Laurie longed to say something tender and comfortable, but no fitting words came to him, so he stood silent, gently stroking her bent head. It was the best thing he could have done; far more soothing than the most eloquent words, for Jo felt the unspoken sympathy and, in the silence, learned the sweet solace which affection administers to sorrow.

"Thank you, Teddy; I'm better now; I don't feel so forlorn, and will try to bear it if it comes."

"Keep hoping for the best; that will help you lots, Jo. Soon your mother will be here, and then everything will be right."

"I'm so glad father is better; now she won't feel so bad about leaving him. Oh, me? it does seem as if all the troubles came in a heap, and I got the heaviest part on my shoulders," sighed Jo.

"Poor girl! you're worn out. Stop a bit I'll hearten you up in a jiffy."

Laurie went off two stairs at a time, and Jo laid her wearied head down on Beth's little brown hood, which no one had thought of moving from the table where she had left it. It must have possessed some magic, for the submissive spirit of its gentle owner seemed to enter into Jo; and when Laurie came running down with a glass of wine, she took it with a smile, and said bravely. "I drink — health to my Beth! You are a good doctor, Teddy, and *such* a comfortable friend; how can I ever pay you?"

"I'll send in my bill, by-and-by; and to-night I'll give you something that will warm the cockles of your heart better than quarts of wine," said Laurie.

"What is it?" cried Jo.

"I telegraphed to your mother yesterday, and Brooke answered she'd come at once; and she'll be here tonight, and everything will be all right."

Laurie spoke very fast, and turned red and excited all in a minute, for he had kept his plot a secret, for fear of disappointing the girls or harming Beth. Jo grew quite white, flew out of her chair, and the moment he stopped speaking she electrified him by throwing her arms round his neck, and crying out, "Oh, Laurie! Oh, mother! I *am* so glad!" She did not weep again, but laughed hysterically, and trembled and clung to her friend as if she was a little bewildered by the sudden news. Laurie, though decidedly amazed, behaved with great presence of mind; he patted her back soothingly, and, finding that she was recovering, followed it up by a bashful kiss or two, which brought Jo round at once. Holding on to the banisters, she put him gently away, saying breathlessly, "Oh, don't! I didn't mean to; it was dreadful of me; but you were such a dear to go and do it, in spite of Hannah, that I couldn't help flying at you. Tell me all about it, and don't give me wine again; it makes me act so."

"I don't mind!" laughed Laurie, as he settled his tie. "Why, you see I got fidgety, and so did grandpa. We thought Hannah was overdoing the authority business, and your mother ought to know. She'd never forgive us if Beth, — well, if anything happened, you know. So I got grandpa to say it was high time we did something, and off I pelted to the office yesterday, for the doctor looked sober, and Hannah most took my head off when I proposed a telegram. Your mother will come, I know, and the train is in at two a.m. I shall go for her; and you've only got to bottle up your rapture, and keep Beth quiet, till that blessed lady gets here."

"Laurie, you're an angel! How shall I ever thank you?"

"Fly at me again; I rather like it," said Laurie, looking mischievous.

151

"No, thank you. I'll do it by proxy, when your grandpa comes. Don't tease, but go home and rest, for you'll be up half the night. Bless you, Teddy, bless you!"

"That's the interferingest chap I ever see; but I forgive him, and do hope Mrs. March is coming on right away," said Hannah, with an air of relief, when Jo told the good news.

Meg had a quiet rapture, while Jo set the sick-room in order, and Hannah "knocked up a couple of pies, in case of company unexpected." A breath of fresh air seemed to blow through the house, and something better that sunshine brightened the quiet rooms; everything appeared to feel the hopeful change; Beth's bird began to chirp again, and a half-blown rose was discovered on Amy's bush on the window; the fires seemed to burn with unusual cheeriness, and every time the girls met, their pale faces broke into smiles as they hugged one another, whispering encouragingly, "Mother's coming, dear! mother's coming!" Everyone rejoiced but Beth; she lay in that heavy stupor, alike unconscious of hope and joy. It was a piteous sight, — the once rosy face so changed and vacant, — the once busy hands so weak and wasted, — the once smiling lips quite dumb, — and the once pretty, well-kept hair scattered rough and tangled on the pillow. All day she lay so, only rousing now and then to mutter, "Water!" with lips so parched they could hardly shape the word; all day Jo and Meg hovered over her, watching, waiting, hoping, and trusting in God and mother; and all day the snow fell, the bitter wind raged, and the hours dragged slowly by. But night came at last; and every time the clock struck, the sisters, still sitting on either side of the bed, looked at each other with brightening eyes, for each hour brought health nearer. The doctor had been in to say that some change for the better or worse would probably take place about midnight, at which time he would return.

Hannah, quite worn out, lay down on the sofa at the bed's foot, and fell fast asleep; Mr. Laurence marched to and fro in the parlour, feeling that he would rather face a rebel battery than Mrs. March's anxious countenance as she entered; Laurie lay on the rug, pretending to rest.

The girls never forgot that night, for no sleep came to them as they kept their watch.

"If God spares Beth, I never will complain again," whispered Meg earnestly.

"If God spares Beth, I'll try to love and serve Him all my life," answered Jo, with equal fervour.

Here the clock struck twelve, and both forgot themselves in watching Beth, for they fancied a change passed over her wan face. The house was still as death. Weary Hannah slept on, and no one but the sisters saw the pale shadow which seemed to fall upon the little bed. An hour went by, and nothing happened except Laurie's quiet departure for the station. Another hour — still no one came; and the anxious fears of delay in the storm, or accidents by the way, or, worst of all, a great grief at Washington, haunted the poor girls.

It was past two when Jo, who stood at the window, heard a movement by the bed, and, turning quickly, saw Meg kneeling before their mother's easy chair, with her face hidden. A dreadful fear passed coldly over Jo, as she thought, "Beth is dead, and Meg is afraid to tell me."

She was back at her post in an instant, and to her excited eyes a great change seemed to have taken place. The fever-flush and the look of pain were gone, and the beloved little face looked so pale and peaceful in its utter repose that Jo felt no desire to weep or lament. Leaning low over this dearest of her sisters, she kissed the damp forehead, and softly whispered, "Good-bye, my Beth; good-bye!"

As if waked by the stir, Hannah started out of her sleep, hurried to the bed, looked at Beth, felt her hands, listened at her lips, and then, throwing her apron over her head, sat down to rock to and fro, exclaiming, "The fever's turned; she's sleepin' natural; her skin's damp; and she breathes easily. Praise be given! Oh, my goodness me!"

Before the girls could believe the happy truth, the doctor came to confirm it. "Yes, my dears, I think the little girl will pull through. Keep the house quiet; let her sleep; and when she wakes give her —"

What they were to give neither heard; for both crept into the dark hall, and, sitting on the stairs, held each other close, rejoicing with hearts too full for words. When they went back to be kissed and cuddled by faithful Hannah, they found Beth lying as she used to do, with her cheek pillowed on her hand, the dreadful pallor gone, and breathing quietly, as if just fallen asleep.

"If mother would only come now," said Jo.

"See," said Meg, coming up with a white, half-opened rose, "I thought this would hardly be ready to lay in Beth's hand tomorrow if she — went away from us. But it has blossomed in the night, and now I mean to put it in my vase here, so that when the darling wakes, the first thing she sees will be the little rose and mother's face."

Never had the sun risen so beautifully, and never had the world seemed so lovely, as it did to the heavy eyes of Meg and Jo, as they looked out in the early morning, when their long, sad vigil was done.

"It looks like a fairy world," said Meg, smiling to herself, as she stood behind the curtain watching the dazzling sight.

"Hark!" cried Jo, starting to her feet.

Yes, there was a sound of bells at the door below, a cry from Hannah, and then Laurie's voice, saying in a joyful whisper, "Girls! she's come!"

## CHAPTER NINETEEN

## AMY'S WILL

While these things were happening at home, Amy was having hard times at Aunt March's. She felt her exile deeply, and, for the first time in her life, realised how much she was beloved and petted at home. Aunt March never petted anyone; but she meant to be kind, for the well-behaved little girl pleased her very much. She did her best to make Amy happy; but, dear me, what mistakes she made! She worried Amy most to death with her rules and orders, her prim ways, and long, prosy talks. Finding the child more docile than her sister, the old lady felt it her duty to try and counteract, as far as possible, the bad effects of home and freedom and indulgence. She took Amy in hand, and taught her as she herself had been taught sixty years ago.

She had to wash the cups every morning, and polish up the old-fashioned spoons, the fat silver teapot, and the glasses till they shone. Then she must dust the room, and what a trying job that was! Not a speck escaped Aunt March's eye, and all the furniture had clawlegs, and much carving, which was never dusted to suit. Then Polly must be fed, the lap-dog combed, and a dozen trips upstairs and down, to get things or deliver orders. After these tiresome labours she must do her lessons. Then she was allowed one hour for exercise or play, and didn't enjoy it! Laurie came, every day, and wheedled Aunt March till Amy was allowed to go out with him, when they walked and rode and had capital times. After dinner she had to read aloud, and sit still while the old lady slept. Then patchwork or towels appeared, and Amy sewed with outward meekness and inward rebellion till dusk, when she was allowed to amuse herself as she liked till tea-time.

If it had not been for Laurie and old Esther, the maid, she felt that she never could have got through that dreadful time. The cook was bad-tempered, the old coachman deaf, and Esther the only one who ever took any notice of the young lady.

Esther was a French woman, who had lived with "Madame," as she called her mistress, for many years. Her real name was Estelle; but Aunt March ordered her to change it, and she obeyed, on condition that she was never asked to change her religion. She took a fancy to Mademoiselle, and amused her with odd stories of her life in France. She also allowed her to roam about the great house, and examine the curious and pretty things stored away in the big wardrobes and the ancient chests; for Aunt March hoarded like a magpie. Amy's chief delight was an Indian cabinet full of queer drawers, like pigeon-holes, and secret places in which were kept all sorts of ornaments. To examine those things gave Amy great satisfaction, especially the jewel cases; in which, on velvet cushions, reposed the ornaments which had adorned a belle forty years ago.

"Which would Mademoiselle choose if she had her will?" asked Esther.

"I should choose this if I might," replied Amy, looking with great admiration at a string of gold and ebony beads, from which hung a heavy cross of the same.

"I, too, covet that. It is a rosary, and as such I should use it like a good Catholic," said Esther.

"Is it meant to use as you use the string of good-smelling wooden beads hanging over your glass?" asked Amy.

"Truly, yes — to pray with."

"You seem to take a deal of comfort in your prayers, Esther, and always come down looking quiet and satisfied. I wish I could."

156

"If Mademoiselle was a Catholic, she would find true comfort; but, as that is not to be, it would be well if you went apart each day to meditate, and pray, as did the good mistress whom I served before Madame. She had a little chapel, and in it found solacement for much trouble."

"Would it be right for me to do so too?" asked Amy, who, in her loneliness, felt the need of help of some sort.

"It would be excellent, and I shall gladly arrange the little dressing-room for you. Say nothing to Madame, but when she sleeps go you and sit alone for a while to think good thoughts, and ask the dear God to preserve your sister."

Amy liked the idea, and gave her leave to arrange the light closet next her room.

"I wish I knew where all these pretty things would go when Aunt March dies," she said, as she slowly replaced the shining rosary and shut the jewel cases one by one.

"To you and your sisters. I know it; Madame confides in me; I witnessed her will, and it is to be so," whispered Esther, smiling.

"How nice! but I wish she'd let us have them now. Procrastination is not agreeable."

"It is too soon yet for the young ladies to wear these things. The first one who is affianced will have the pearls — Madame has said it; and I have a fancy that the little turquoise ring will be given to you when you go, for Madame approves your good behaviour and charming manners."

"Do you think so? Oh, I'll be a lamb, if I can only have that lovely ring! It's ever so much prettier than Kitty Bryant's. I do like Aunt March, after all," and Amy tried on the blue ring with a delighted face.

From that day she was a model of obedience, and the old lady admired the success of her training. Esther fitted up the closet with a little table, placed a footstool before it, and over it a picture. It was a valuable copy of one of the famous pictures of the world, and Amy's beauty-loving eyes were never tired of looking up at the sweet face of the divine mother, while tender thoughts of her own were busy at her heart. On the table she laid her little Testament and hymn-book, kept a vase always full of the best flowers Laurie brought her, and came every day to "sit alone, thinking good thoughts, and praying the dear God to preserve her sister."

She tried to forget herself, to keep cheerful, and be satisfied with doing right. In her first effort at being good, she decided to make her will, as Aunt March had done. It cost her a pang even to think of giving up the little treasures which in her eyes were as precious as the old lady's jewels.

During one of her play hours she wrote out the important document, with some help from Esther, as to certain legal terms; and when the good-natured French woman had signed her name, Amy felt relieved, and laid it by to show Laurie, whom she wanted as a second witness. As it was a rainy day, she went upstairs to amuse herself in one of the large chambers, and took Polly with her for company. In this room there was a wardrobe full of old-fashioned costumes, and it was her favourite amusement to array herself in the faded brocades, and parade up and down before the long mirror, making stately curtsies, and sweeping her train about with a rustle which delighted her ears. So busy was she on this day that she did not hear Laurie's ring, nor see his face peeping in at her, as she gravely promenaded to and fro, flirting her fan and tossing her head, on which she wore a great pink turban. She was obliged to walk carefully, for she had on high-heeled shoes, and, as Laurie told Jo afterward, it was a comical sight to see her mince along, with Polly brindling just behind her, imitating her as well as he could, and stopping to laugh or exclaim, "Ain't we fine? Get along, you fright! Hold your tongue. Kiss me, dear; ha! ha!"

Having with difficulty restrained an explosion of merriment, Laurie tapped, and was graciously received.

"Sit down and rest while I put these things away; then I want to consult you about a very serious matter," said Amy, when she had shown her splendour, and driven Polly into a corner. "That bird is the trial of my life," she continued, removing the pink mountain from her head, while Laurie seated himself astride a chair.

"I'd wring your neck if you were mine, you old torment!" cried Laurie, shaking his fist at the bird, who put his head on one side, and gravely croaked, "Allyluyer! bless your buttons, dear!"

"Nod I'm ready," said Amy, shutting the wardrobe, and taking a paper out of her pocket. "I want you to read that, please, and tell me if it is legal. I fear that I ought to do it, for life is uncertain, and I don't want any ill-feeling over my tomb."

Laurie bit his lips, and turning a little from the pensive speaker, read the following document with praiseworthy gravity:

### "MY LAST WILL AND TESTAMENT

"I, Amy Curtis March, being in my sane mind, do give and bequeethe all my personal property — viz. to wit: — namely, —

"To my father, my best pictures, sketches, maps, and works of art, including frames. Also my $ 100, to do what he likes with.

"To my mother, all my clothes, except the blue apron with pockets — also my likeness, and my medal, with much love.

"To my dear sister Margaret, I give my turquoise ring (if I get it), also my green box with the doves on it, also my piece of real lace for her neck, and my sketch of her as a memorial of her 'little girl.' "

To Jo I leave my breast-pin, the one mended with sealing-wax, also my bronze inkstand — she lost the cover — and my most precious plaster rabbit, because I am sorry I burnt up her story.

"To Beth I give my dolls and the little bureau, my fan, my linen collars and my new slippers. And herewith also leave her my regret that I ever made fun of old Joanna.

"To my friend and neighbour Theodore Laurence I bequeath my paper marshay portfolio, my clay model of a horse, though he did say it hadn't any neck. Also in return for his great kindness in the hour of affliction any one of my artistic works he likes, Noter Dame is the best.

"To our venerable benefactor Mr. Laurence I leave my purple box with a looking glass in the cover which will be nice for his pens and remind him of the departed girl who thanks him for his favours to her family, specially Beth.

"I wish my favourite playmate Kitty Bryant to have the blue silk apron and my gold-bead ring with a kiss.

"To Hannah I gave the band-box she wanted and all the patchwork I leave hoping she 'will remember me, when it you see.'

"To this will and testament I set my hand and seal on this 20th day of Nov. Anno Domini 1861.

"AMY CURTIS MARCH."

"WITNESSES: {Estelle Valnor,
Theodore Laurence."

"What put it into your head? Did anyone tell you about Beth's giving away her things?" asked Laurence soberly.

She explained; and then asked anxiously, "What about Beth?"

"She felt so ill one day that she told Jo she wanted to give her piano to Meg, her bird to you, and the poor old doll to Jo, who would love it for her sake. She was sorry she had so little to give, and left locks of hair to the rest of us, and her best love to grandpa. *She* never thought of a will."

Laurie was signing and sealing as he spoke, and did not look up till a great tear dropped on the paper. Amy's face was full of trouble; but she only said, "Don't people put sort of postscripts to their wills, sometimes?"

"Yes; 'codicils' they call them."

"Put one in mine then — that I wish *all* my curls cut off, and given round to my friends."

Laurie added it, smiling at Amy's last and greatest sacrifice. Then he amused her for an hour, and was much interested in all her trials. But when he came to go, Amy held him back to whisper, with trembling lips, "Is there really any danger about Beth?"

"I'm afraid there is; but we must hope for the best, so don't cry, dear"; and Laurie put his arm about her with a brotherly gesture which was very comforting.

When he had gone, she went to her little chapel, and prayed for Beth with streaming tears and an aching heart, feeling that a million turquoise rings would not console for the loss of her gentle little sister.

CHAPTER TWENTY

## CONFIDENTIAL

I don't think I have any words in which to tell the meeting of the mother and daughters; such hours are beautiful to live, but very hard to describe, so I will leave it to the imagination of my readers, merely saying that the house was full of genuine happiness, and that Meg's tender hope was realised; for when Beth woke from that long, healing sleep, the first objects on which her eyes fell *were* the little rose and mother's face. Too weak to wonder at anything, she only smiled, and nestled close into the loving arms about her, feeling the hungry longing was satisfied at last. Then she slept again, and the girls waited upon their mother, for she would not unclasp the thin hand which clung to hers, even in sleep. Hannah had "dished up" an astonishing breakfast for the traveller; and Meg and Jo fed their mother like dutiful storks, while they listened to her account of father's state, Mr. Brooke's promise to stay and nurse him, the delays which the storm occasioned on the homeward journey, and the comfort Laurie's hopeful face had given her when she arrived, worn out with fatigue, anxiety, and cold.

What a strange, yet pleasant day that was! so brilliant and gay without, for all the world seemed abroad to welcome the first snow; so quiet and reposeful within, for everyone slept, spent with watching. With a blissful sense of burdens lifted off, Meg and Jo closed their weary eyes, and lay at rest. Mrs. March would not leave Beth's side, but rested in the big chair, waking often to look at, touch, and brood over her child, like a miser over recovered treasure.

Laurie, meanwhile, posted off to comfort Amy, and told his story so well that Aunt March actually "sniffed" herself, and never once said "I told you so," Amy came out so strong on this occasion that the good thoughts in the little chapel really began to bear fruit. She dried her tears quickly, restrained her impatience to see her mother, and never even thought of the turquoise ring, when the old lady heartily agreed in Laurie's opinion, that she behaved "like a capital little woman." She would gladly have gone out to enjoy the bright wintry weather, but, discovering that Laurie was dropping with sleep, she persuaded him to rest on the sofa, while she wrote a note to her mother. She was a long time about it; and, when she returned, he was stretched out with both arms under his head, sound asleep, while Aunt March had pulled down the curtains and sat doing nothing in an unusual fit of benignity.

After a while, they began to think he was not going to wake till night, and I'm not sure that he would, had he not been effectually roused by Amy's cry of joy at sight of her mother. There probably were a good many happy little girls in and about the city that day, but it is my private opinion that Amy was the happiest of all, when she sat in her mother's lap and told her trials, receiving consolation and compensation in the shape of approving smiles and fond caresses. They were alone together in the chapel, to which her mother did not object when its purpose was explained to her.

"On the contrary, I like it very much, dear," she said. "It is an excellent plan to have some place where we can go to be quiet when things grieve us."

"Yes, mother; and when I go home I mean to have a corner in the big closet to put my books, and the copy of that picture which I've tried to make. The woman's face is not good, it's too beautiful for me to draw, but the baby is done better, and I love it very much."

As Amy pointed to the smiling Christ-child on the mother's knee, Mrs. March saw something on the lifted hand that made her smile. She said nothing, but Amy understood the look, and, after a minute's pause, she added gravely, "I wanted to speak to you about this. Aunt gave me the ring today; she called me to her and kissed me, and put it on my finger, and said I was a credit to her. She gave that funny guard to keep the turquoise on, as it's too big. I'd like to wear them, mother, can I?"

"They are very pretty, but I think you're rather too young for such ornaments, Amy," said Mrs. March.

163

"I'll try not to be vain," said Amy; "I don't think I like it only because it's so pretty; but I want to wear it as the girl in the story wore her bracelet; to remind me of something.'

"Do you mean Aunt March?" asked her mother, laughing

"No, to remind me not to be selfish. I've thought a great deal lately about 'my bundle of naughties,' and being selfish is the largest one in it. Beth isn't selfish, and that's the reason everyone loves her. People wouldn's feel half so bad about me if I was sick; but I'd like to be loved, and missed by a great many friends so I'm going to try to be like Beth. I'm apt to forget my resolutions; but, if I had something always about to remind me, I guess I should do better. My I try this way?"

"Yes; but I have more faith in the corner of the big closet. Wear your ring, dear, and do your best; I think you will prosper, for the sincere wish to be good is half the battle. Now I must go back to Beth. Keep up your heart, little daughter, and we will soon have you home again."

That evening, while Meg was writing to her father, to report the traveller's safe arrival, Jo slipped upstairs into Beth's room, and, finding her mother in her usual place, stood a minute twisting her fingers in her hair, with a worried gesture.

"What is it deary?" asked Mrs. March.

"I want to tell you something, mother."

"About Meg?"

"How quick you guessed! Yes, it's about her; and, though it's a little thing, it fidgets me."

"Beth is asleep; speak low, and tell me all about it. That Moffat hasn't been here, I hope?" asked Mrs. March, rather sharply.

"No; I should have shut the door in his face if he had, said Jo, settling herself on the floor at her mother's feet. "Last summer Meg left a pair of gloves over at the Laurence's and only one was returned. We forgot all about it till **Teddy** told me that Mr. Brooke had it. He kept it in his waistcoat pocket, and once it fell out, and Teddy joked him about it, and Mr. Brooke owned that he liked Meg, but didn't dare say so, she was so young and he so poor. Now, isn't it a *dreadful* state of things?"

"Do you think Meg cares for him?" asked Mrs. March with an anxious look.

"Mercy me! I don't know anything about love and such nonsense!" cried Jo, with a funny mixture of interest and contempt. "In novels the girls show it by starting and blushing, fainting away, growing thin, and acting like fools. Now Meg don't do anything of the sort; she eats and drinks, and sleeps, like a sensible creature; she looks straight in my face when I talk about that man, and only blushes a little bit when Teddy jokes about lovers."

"Then you fancy that Meg is *not* interested in John ?"

"Who?" cried Jo, staring.

"Mr. Brooke; I call him 'John' now; we fell into the way of doing so at the hospital."

"Oh, dear! I know you'll take his part; he's been so good to father, and you won't send him away, but let Meg marry him. Mean thing! to go petting pa and trucking to you, just to wheedle you into liking him."

"My dear, don't get angry about this. John went with me at Mr. Laurence's request, and was so devoted to poor father that we couldn't help getting fond of him. He was perfectly honourable about Meg, for he told us he loved her, but would earn a comfortable home before he asked her to marry him. He only wanted our leave to love her and work for her. He is a truly excellent young man, and we could not refuse to listen to him; but I will not consent to Meg's engaging herself so young."

165

"Of course not, it would be idiotic! I knew there was mischief brewing; I felt it; and now it's worse than I imagined. I just wish I could marry Meg myself and keep her safe in the family."

This odd arrangement made Mrs. March smile, but she said gravely, "Jo, I confide in you, and don't wish you to say anything to Meg yet. When John comes back, and I see them together, I can judge better of her feelings towards him."

"She'll see his in those handsome eyes that she talks about, and then it will be all up with her. She's got such a soft heart, it will melt like butter in the sun if anyone looks sentimentally at her. She read the short reports he sent more than she did your letters, and pinched me when I spoke of it, and likes brown eyes, and don't think John an ugly name, and she'll go and fall in love, and there's an end of peace, and fun, and cosy times together. Oh, deary me; why weren't we all boys? then there wouldn't be any bother!"

Jo leaned her chin on her knees in a disconsolate attitude and shook her fist at the reprehensible John. Mrs. March sighed, and Jo looked up with an air of relief.

"You don't like it mother? I'm glad of it; let's send him about his business, and not tell Meg a word of it, but all be jolly together."

"I did wrong to sigh, Jo. It is natural and right you should all go to homes of your own in time; but I do want to keep my gilrs as long as I can, and I am sorry that this happened so soon, for Meg is only seventeen. Your father and I have agreed that she shall not bind herself, nor be married before twenty. If she and John love one another, they can wait, and test the love by doing so."

"Hadn't you rather have her marry a rich man?" asked Jo.

"Money is a good and useful thing, Jo, and I hope my girls will never feel the need of it too bitterly, nor be tempted by too much. I am content to see Meg begin humbly, for she will be rich in the possession of a good man's heart, and that is better than a fortune."

"I understand, mother; but I'm disappointed about Meg, for I'd planned to have her marry Teddy by-and-by, and sit in the lap of luxury all her days. Wouldn't it be nice?" asked Jo, looking up with a brighter face.

"He is younger than she, you know," began Mrs. March, but Jo broke in, —

"Oh, that don't matter; he's old for his age, and tall. Then he's rich and generous, and good, and loves us all."

"I'm afraid Laurie is hardly grown-up enough for Meg, and altogether too much of a weather-cock, just now, for anyone to depend on. Don't make plans, Jo; but let time and their hearts mate your friends. We can't meddle safely in such matters, and had better not get 'romantic rubbish', as you call it, into our heads, lest it spoil our friendship."

"Well, I won't; but I hate to see things going all criss-cross and getting snarled up, when a pull here, and a snip there, would straighten it out, I wish wearing flat-irons on our heads would keep us from growing up. But buds will be roses, and kittens, cats — more's the pity!"

"What's that about flat-irons and cats?" asked Meg, as she crept into the room with the finished letter in her hand.

"Only one of my stupid speeches. I'm going to bed; come on, Peggy," said Jo, unfolding herself, like an animated puzzle.

"Quite right, and beautifully written. Please add that I send my love to John," said Mrs. March, as she glanced over the letter.

"Do you call him 'John?'" asked Meg smiling.

"Yes; he has been like a son to us, and we are very fond of him," replied Mrs. March.

"I'm glad of that; he is so lonely. Good-night, mother, dear. It is so comfortable to have you here," was Meg's quiet answer.

The kiss her mother gave her was a very tender one, and, as she went away, Mrs. March said, with a mixture of satisfaction and regret, "She does not love John, yet, but will soon learn to."

## CHAPTER TWENTY-ONE

# LAURIE MAKES MISCHIEF, AND JO MAKES PEACE

Jo's face was a study next day, for the secret rather weighed upon her, and she found it hard not to look mysterious. Meg observed it, but did not trouble to make inquiries, for she had learned that the best way to manage Jo was by the law of contraries; so she felt sure of being told everything if she did not ask. She was surprised, therefore, when the silence remained unbroken, and Jo assumed a patronising air, which aggravated Meg, who, in her turn, assumed an air of dignified reserve, and devoted herself to her mother. This left Jo to her own devices; for Mrs. March had taken her place as nurse. Amy being gone, Laurie was her only refuge; and much as she enjoyed his society, she rather dreaded him just then, for she feared he would coax her secret from her.

She was quite right; for the mischief-loving lad no sooner suspected a mystery than he settled himself to finding it out. At last, by dint of perseverance, he satisfied himself that it concerned Meg and Mr. Brooke. Feeling indignant that he was not taken into his tutor's confidence, he set his wits to work to devise some proper retaliation.

Meg, meanwhile, was absorbed in preparations for her father's return, but all of a sudden a change seemed to come over her, and, for a day or two, she was quite unlike herself. She started when spoken to, blushed when looked at, and sat over her sewing with a timid, troubled look on her face. To her mother's inquiries she answered that she was quite well, and Jo's she silenced by begging to be let alone.

"She feels it in the air — love, I mean. She's got most of the symptoms, is twittery and cross, don't eat, lies awake, and mopes in corners. I caught her singing that song about 'the silver-voiced brook,' and once she said 'John,' as you do, and then turned as red as a poppy. Whatever shall we do?" said Jo.

"Nothing but wait; let her alone, be kind and patient, and father's coming will settle everything," replied her mother.

"Here's a note to you, Meg, all sealed up. How odd! Teddy never seals mine," said Jo, next day, as she distributed the contents of the little post-office.

Mrs. March and Jo were deep in their own affairs when a sound from Meg made them look up to see her staring at her note with a frightened face.

"My child, what is it?" cried her mother, running to her, while Jo tried to take the paper which had done the mischief.

"It's all a mistake — he didn't send it — oh, Jo, how could you do it?" and Meg hid her face in her hands, crying as if her heart was quite broken.

"Me! I've done nothing! What's she talking about?" cried Jo, bewildered.

Meg's mild eyes kindled with anger as she pulled a crumpled note from her pocket, and threw it at Jo, saying reproachfully, —

"You wrote it and that bad boy helped you. How could you be so rude, so mean, and cruel to us both?"

Jo hardly heard her, for she and her mother were reading the note, which was written in a peculiar hand.

"My Dearest Margaret, — I can no longer restrain my passion, and must know my fate before I return. I dare not tell your parents yet, but I think they would consent if they knew that we adored one another. Mr. Laurence will help me to some good place, and then, my sweet girl, you will make me happy. I implore you to say nothing to your family yet, but to send one word of hope through Laurie to

"*Your devoted,*
"*John.*"

"Oh, the little villain! that's the way he meant to pay me for keeping my word to mother. I'll give him a hearty scolding, and bring him over to beg pardon," cried Jo, burning to execute immediate justice. But her mother held her back, saying, with a look she seldom wore.

"Stop, Jo; you must clear yourself first. You have played so many pranks that I am afraid you have had a hand in this."

"On my word, mother, I haven't! I never saw that note before," said Jo, so earnestly that they believed her." If I *had* taken a part in it, I'd have done it better that this, and have written a sensible note."

"It's like his writing," faltered Meg, comparing it with the note in her hand.

"Hush! let me manage this, for it is worse than I thought. Margaret, tell me the whole story," commanded Mrs. March, sitting down by Meg.

"I received the first letter from Laurie, who didn't look as if he knew anything about it," began Meg, without looking up. "I was worried at first, and meant to tell you; then, I remembered how you liked Mr. Brooke, so I thought you wouldn't mind if I kept my little secret for a few days. Forgive me, mother; I'm paid for my silliness now. I never can look him in the face again."

"What did you say to him?" asked Mrs. March.

"I only said I was too young to do anything about it yet; that I didn't wish to have secrets from you, and he must speak to father. I was very grateful for his kindness, and would be his friend, but nothing more, for a long while."

Mrs. March smiled, as if well pleased, and Jo clapped her hands, exclaiming with a laugh, —

"You are almost equal to Caroline Percy, who was a pattern of prudence! Tell on, Meg. What did he say to that?"

"He writes in a different way entirely, telling me that he never sent any love-letter at all, and is very sorry that my roguish sister, Jo, should take liberties with our names. It's very kind and respectful, but think how dreadful for me!"

Meg leaned against her mother, looking the image of despair, and Jo tramped about the room, calling Laurie names. All of a sudden she stopped, caught up the two notes, and, after looking at them closely, said decidedly, "I don't believe Brooke ever saw either of these letters. Teddy wrote both, and keeps yours to crow over me with, because I wouldn't tell him my secret."

"Don't have any secrets, Jo; tell it to mother, and keep out of trouble, as I should have done," said Meg warningly.

"Bless you, child!" mother told me.

"That will do, Jo. I'll comfort Meg while you go and get Laurie. I shall sift the matter to the bottom, and put a stop to such pranks at once."

Away ran Jo, and Mrs. March gently told Meg Mr. Brooke's real feelings. "Now, dear, what are your own? Do you love him enough to wait till he can make a home for you, or will you keep yourself quite free for the present?"

"I've been so scared and worried, I don't want to have anything to do with lovers for a long while — perhaps never," answered Meg petulantly. "If John *doesn't* know anything about this nonsense, don't tell him, and make Jo and Laurie hold their tongues. I won't be deceived and plagued and made a fool of — it's a shame!"

Seeing that Meg's usually gentle temper was roused, and her pride hurt by this mischievous joke, Mrs. March soothed her by promises of entire silence. The instant Laurie's step was heard in the hall, Meg fled into the study, and Mrs. March received the culprit alone. Jo had not told him why he was wanted; but he knew the minute he saw Mrs. March's face, and stood twirling his hat with a guilty air. Jo was dismissed, and chose to march up and down the hall like a sentinel, having some fear that the prisoner might bolt. The sound of voices in the parlour rose and fell for half an hour; but what happened during that interview the girls never knew.

When they were called in, Laurie was standing by their mother with such a penitent face that Jo forgave him on the spot. Meg received his apology, and was much comforted by the assurance that Brooke knew nothing of the joke.

"I'll never tell him to my dying day, wild horses shan't drag it out of me; so you'll forgive me, Meg, and I'll do anything to show how out-and-out sorry I am," he added, looking very much ashamed.

"I'll try; but it was a very ungentlemanly thing to do. I didn't think you could be so sly and malicious, Laurie," replied Meg.

"It was altogether abominable, and I don't deserve to be spoken to for a month; but you will, though, won't you?" and Laurie folded his hands together, with such an imploring gesture, and rolled up his eyes in such a repentant way as he spoke in his persuasive tone, that it was impossible to frown upon him. Meg pardoned him, and Mrs. March's grave face relaxed.

Jo stood aloof, trying to harden her heart against him, and succeeding only in primming up her face into an expression of entire disapprobation. Laurie looked at her once or twice, but, as she showed no signs of relenting, he felt injured and turned his back on her till the others were done with him, when he made her a low bow, and walked off without a word.

As soon as he had gone, she wished she had been more forgiving; and, when Meg and her mother went upstairs, she felt lonely and longed for Teddy. After resisting for some time, she yielded to the impulse and went over to the big house.

"Is Mr. Laurence in?" asked Jo, of a housemaid, who was coming downstairs.

"Yes, miss; but I don't believe he's seeable yet."

"Why not? Is he ill?"

"La, no, miss! but he's had a scene with Mr. Laurie, who is in one of his tantrums about something, which vexes the old gentleman, so I dursn't go nigh him."

"Where is Laurie?"

"Shut up in his room, and he won't answer. I don't know what's to come of the dinner."

"I'll go and see what the matter is. I'm not afraid of either of them."

Up went Jo, and knocked smartly on the door of Laurie's little study.

"Stop that, or I'll open the door and make you!" called out the young gentleman.

Jo pounded again; the door flew open, and in she bounced before Laurie could recover from his surprise. Seeing that he really was out of temper, Jo assumed a contrite expression, and going down upon her knees, said meekly, "Please forgive me for being so cross. I came to make it up."

"It's all right; get up, and don't be a goose, Jo," was the cavalier reply to her petition.

"Thank you; I will. Could I ask what's the matter?"

"I've been shaken, and I won't bear it!" growled Laurie indignantly.

"Who did it?" demanded Jo.

"Grandfather; if it had been anyone else I'd have —" and the injured youth finished his sentence by an energetic gesture of the right arm.

"That's nothing; I often shake you, and you don't mind," said Jo, soothingly.

"Pooh! you're a girl; and it's fun; but I'll allow no man to shake *me*."

"I don't think anyone would care to try it, if you looked as much like a thunder-cloud as you do now. Why were you treated so?"

"Just because I wouldn't say what your mother wanted me for. I'd promised not to tell, and of course I wasn't going to break my word."

"Couldn't you satisfy your grandpa in any other way?"

"No; he *would* have the truth. I'd have told my part of the scrape, if I could without bringing Meg in. As I couldn't, I held my tongue, and bore the scolding till the old gentleman collared me. Then I got angry, and bolted, for fear I should forget myself."

"It wasn't nice, but he's sorry I know; so go down and make up. I'll help you."

"Hanged if I do! I'm not going to be lectured and pummelled by everyone, just for a bit of a frolic; *I was* sorry about Meg, and begged pardon like a man; but I won't do it again, when I wasn't in the wrong."

174

"He didn't know that."

"He ought to trust me, and not act as if I was a baby. It's no use, Jo; he's got to learn that I'm able to take care of myself, and don't need anyone's apron-string to hold on by."

"What pepper-pots you are!" sighed Jo. "How do you mean to settle this affair?"

"Well, he ought to beg pardon, and believe me when I say I can't tell him what the row's about."

"Bless you! he won't do that."

"I won't go down till he does."

"Now, Teddy, be sensible; let it pass, and I'll explain what I can. You can't stay here, so what's the use of being melodramatic?"

"I don't intend to stay here long, anyway. I'll slip off and take a journey somewhere, and when grandpa misses me, he'll come round fast enough."

"I dare say; but you ought not to go and worry him."

"Don't preach. I'll go to Washington and see Brooke; it's gay there."

"What fun you'd have! I wish I could run off too!" said Jo, forgetting her part of the Mentor in lively visions of martial life at the capital.

"Come on, then! Why not? You go and surprise your father. It would be a glorious joke; let's do it, Jo! We'll leave a letter saying we are all right, and trott of at once."

For a moment Jo looked as if she would agree; for, wild as the plan was, it just suited her. She was tired of care and confinement, longed for change, and thoughts of her father blended temptingly with the novel charms of camps and hospitals, liberty and fun. Her eyes kindled as they turned wistfully towards the window; but they fell on the old house opposite, and she shook her head with sorrowful decision.

"If I was a boy, we'd run away together, and have a capital time; but as I'm a miserable girl, I must be proper and stop at home. Don't tempt me Teddy; it's a crazy plan."

"That's the fun of it!" began Laurie.

"Hold your tongue!" cried Jo, covering her ears.

"I knew Meg would wet-blanket such a proposal but I thought you had more spirit," began Laurie.

"Bad boy, be quiet. Sit down and think of your own sins; don't go making me add to mine. If I get your grandpa to apologize for the shaking, will you give up running away?" asked Jo.

"Yes; but you won't do it," answered Laurie.

"If I can manage the young one, I can the old man," muttered Jo, as she walked away.

"Come in," and Mr. Laurence's gruff voice sounded gruffer than ever as Jo tapped his door.

"It's only me, sir, come to return a book," she said blandly as she entered.

"Want any more?" asked the old gentleman, looking grim and vexed, but trying not to show it.

"Yes, please; I like old Sam so well I think I'll try the second volume," returned Jo, hoping to propitiate him by accepting a second dose of Boswell's Johnson, as he had recommended that lively work.

The shaggy eyebrow unbent a little as he rolled the steps towards the shelf where the Johnsonian literature was placed. Jo skipped up, and, sitting on the top step, affected to be searching for her book, but was really wondering how best to introduce the dangerous object of her visit. Mr. Laurence seemed to suspect that something was brewing in her mind;

for, after taking several brisk turns about the room, he faced round on her, speaking so abruptly that Rasselas tumbled face downwards on the floor.

"What has that boy been about? I know he has been in mischief, by the way he acted when he came home. I can't get a .word from him; and when I threatened to shake the truth out of him, he bolted upstairs and locked himself in his room."

"He did do wrong, but we forgave him, and all promised not to say a word to anyone," began Jo reluctantly.

"That won't do; he shall not shelter himself behind a promise from you soft-hearted girls. If he's done anything amiss, he shall confess, beg pardon, and be punished. Out with it, Jo!"

Mr. Laurence looked so alarming, that Jo would have gladly run away, if she could, but she was perched aloft on the steps, and he stood at the foot, a lion in the path; so she had to stay and brave it out.

"Indeed, sir, I cannot tell; mother forbid it. Laurie has confessed, asked pardon, and been punished quite enough. We don't keep silence to shield him, but someone else; and it will make more trouble if you interfere. Please don't; it was partly my fault, but it's right now, so let's forget it, and talk about the *Rambler,* or something pleasant."

"Hand the *Rambler!* Come down and give me your word that this harum-scarum boy of mine hasn't done anything ungrateful or impertinent. If he has, after all your kindness to him, I'll thrash him with my own hands."

The threat sounded awful, but did not alarm Jo, for she knew the irascible old man would never lift a finger against his grandson, whatever he might say to the contrary. She obediently descended, and made as light of the prank as she could without betraying Meg or forgetting the truth.

"Hum! ha! well, if the boy held his tongue because he'd promised, and not from obstinacy, I'll forgive him. He's a stubborn fellow, and hard to manage," said Mr. Laurence.

"So am I; but a kind word will govern me when all the king's horses and all the king's men couldn't," said Jo.

"You think I'm not kind to him, hey?" was the sharp answer.

"Oh, dear, no, sir; you are rather too kind sometimes, and then just a trifle hasty when he tries your patience. Don't you think you are?"

Jo was determined to have it out now, and tried to look quite placid, though she quaked a little after her bold speech. To her great relief, the old gentleman only threw his spectacles on to the table, with a rattle, and exclaimed frankly, — "You're right girl, I am! I love the boy, but he tries my patience past bearing, and I don't know how it will end, if we go on so."

"I'll tell you, he'll run away." Jo was sorry for that speech the minute it was made.

Mr. Laurence's ruddy face changed suddenly, and he sat down with a troubled glance at the picture of a handsome man which hung over his table. It was Laurie's father, who had run away in his youth, and married against the imperious old man's will.

"He won't do it unless he is very much worried, and only threatens it sometimes, when he gets tired of studying. I often think I should like to, especially since my hair was cut; so, if you ever miss us, you may advertise for two boys, and look among the ships bound for India."

178

She laughed as she spoke, and Mr. Laurence looked relieved, evidently taking the whole as a joke.

"You hussy! how dare you talk in that way! Bless the boys and girls! what torments they are; yet we can't do without them," he said, pinching her cheeks good-humouredly.

"Go and bring that boy down to his dinner; tell him it's all right, and advise him not to put on tragedy airs with his grandfather; I won't bear it."

"He won't come, sir; he feels badly because you didn't believe him when he said he couldn't tell. I think the shaking hurt his feelings."

Jo tried to look pathetic, but must have failed, for Mr. Laurence began to laugh.

"I'm sorry for that, and ought to thank him for not shaking me, I suppose. What the dickens does the fellow expect?"

"If I was you, I'd write him an apology, sir. He says he won't come down till he has one. A formal apology will make him see how foolish he is, and bring him down quite amiable. Try it; he likes fun. I'll carry it up and teach him his duty."

Mr. Laurence gave her a sharp look, and put on his spectacles, saying slowly, "You're a sly puss! but I don't mind being managed by you and Beth. Here, give me a bit of paper, and let us have done with this nonsense."

The note was written in the terms which one gentleman would use to another after offering some deep insult. Jo dropped a kiss on the top of Mr. Laurence bald head and ran up to slip the apology under Laurie's door, advising him, through the key-hole, to be submissive, decorous, and a few other agreeable possibilities. Finding the door locked again, she left the note to do its work, and was going quietly away, when the young gentleman, slid down the banisters, and waited for her at the bottom, saying, "What a good fellow you are, Jo! Did you get blown up?"

"No; he was pretty mild, on the whole."

"Ah! I got it all round! Even you case me off over there and I felt just ready to go to the deuce," he began apologetically.

"Don't talk in that way; turn over a new leaf to begin again, Teddy, my son."

"I keep turning over new leaves, and spoiling them," he said dolefully.

"Go and eat your dinner; you'll feel better after it. Men always croak when they are hungry"; and Jo whisked out at the front door after that.

Everyone thought the matter ended, and the little cloud blown over, but the mischief was done, for, though others forgot it, Meg remembered. She never alluded to a certain person, but she thought of him a good deal, dreamed dreams more that ever; and once, Jo, rummaging her sister's desk for stamps, found a bit of paper scribbled over with the words, "Mrs. John Brooke," whereat she groaned, feeling that Laurie's prank had hastened the evil day for her.


CHAPTER TWENTY-TWO

# PLEASANT MEADOWS

Like sunshine after storm were the peaceful weeks which followed. The invalids improved rapidly, and Mr. March began to talk of returning early in the new year. Beth was soon able to lie on the study sofa all day, amusing herself with the well-beloved cats. Her once active limbs were so stiff and feeble that Jo took her a daily airing about the house in her strong arms. Meg cheerfully blackened and burnt her white hands cooking delicate messes for "the dear," while Amy, a loyal slave of the ring, celebrated her return by giving away as many of her treasures as she could prevail on her sisters to accept.

Several days of unusually mild weather fitly ushered in a splendid Christmas Day. Hannah "felt in her bones that it was going to be an uncommonly plummy day," and she proved herself a true prophetess, for everybody and everything seemed bound to produce a grand success. To begin with: Mr. March wrote that he would soon be with them; then Beth felt uncommonly well that morning, and, being dressed in her mother's gift — a soft crimson merino wrapper — was borne in triumph to the window, to behold the offering of Jo and Laurie. Out in the garden stood a stately snow-maiden, crowned with holly, bearing a basket of fruit and flowers in one hand, a great roll of new music in the other, a perfect rainbow of an Afghan round her chilly shoulders, and a Christmas carol issuing from her lips, on a pink paper streamer.

How Beth laughed when she saw it! How Laurie ran up and down to bring in the gifts, and what ridiculous speeches Jo made as she presented them.

"I'm so full of happiness that, if father were only here, I couldn't hold one drop more," said Beth, sighing with contentment, as Jo carried her off the study to rest after the excitement.

"So am I," added Jo, slapping the pocket wherein reposed the long-desired *Undine and Sintram.*

"I'm sure I am," echoed Amy, poring over the engraved copy of the Madonna and Child, which her mother had given her, in a pretty frame.

"Of course I am," cried Meg, smoothing the silvery folds of her first silk dress; for Mr. Laurence had insisted on giving it.

"How can I be otherwise!" said Mrs. March gratefully, as her eyes went from her husband's letter to Beth's smiling face, and her hand caressed the brooch made of grey and golden chestnut and dark brown hair, which the girls had just fastened on her breast.

Half an hour after everyone had said they were so happy they could only hold one drop more, the drop came. Laurie opened the parlour door, and popped his head in very quietly. He might just as well have turned a somersault, and uttered an Indian war-whoop; for his face was so full of suppressed excitement, and his voice so joyful, that everyone jumped up, though he only said, in a queer breathless voice, "Here's another Christmas present for the March family."

Before the words were well out of his mouth, he was whisked away somehow, and in his place appeared a tall man, muffled up to the eyes, leaning on the arm of another tall man. Of course there was a general stampede; and for several minutes everybody seemed to lose their wits, for the strangest things were done, and no one said a word. Mr. March became invisible in the embrace of four pairs of loving arms; Jo disgraced herself by nearly fainting away, and had to be doctored by Laurie in the china closet; Mr. Brooke kissed Meg entirely by mistake, as he somewhat incoherently explained; and Amy, the dignified, tumbled over a stool, and never stopping to get up, hugged and cried over her father's boots in the most touching manner. Mrs. March was the first to recover herself, and held up her hand with a warning, "Hush! remember Beth!"

But it was too late; the study door flew open — the little red wrapper appeared on the threshold — joy put strength into the feeble limbs — and Beth ran straight into her father's arms.

It was not at all romantic, but a hearty laugh set everybody straight again, for Hannah was discovered behind the door, sobbing over the fat turkey, which she had forgotten to put down when she rushed up from the kitchen. As the laugh subsided, Mrs. March began to thank Mr. Brooke for his faithful care of her husband, at which Mr. Brooke suddenly remembered that Mr. March needed rest, and, seizing Laurie he precipitately retired. Then the two invalids were ordered to repose, which they did, by both sitting in one big chair, and talking hard.

Mr. March told how he had longed to surprise them, and how, when the fine weather came, he had been allowed by the doctor to take advantage of it; how devoted Brooke had been and how he was altogether a most estimable young man. Why Mr. March paused just there, and, after a glance at Meg, who was violently poking the fire, looked at his wife with an inquiring lift of the eyebrows, I leave you to imagine; also why Mrs. March gently nodded her head. Jo saw and understood the look; and she stalked grimly away to get wine and beef tea, muttering to herself, "I hate estimable young men with brown eyes!"

There never *was* such a Christmas dinner as they had that day. The fat turkey was a sight to behold, when Hannah sent him up, stuffed, browned, and decorated. So was the plum-pudding, which melted in one's mouth; likewise the jellies. Everything turned out well; which was a mercy, Hannah said, "For my mind was that flustered, mum, that it's a miracle I didn't roast the pudding, and stuff the turkey with raisins, let alone bilin'it in a cloth."

Mr. Laurence and his grandson dined with them; also Mr. Brooke, at whom Jo glowered darkly, to Laurie's infinite amusement. Two easychairs stood side by side at the head of the table, in which sat Beth and her father feasting, modestly, on chicken and a little fruit. They drank healths, told stories, sung songs, "reminisced," and had a thoroughly good time. A sleigh-ride had been planned, but the girls would not leave their father; so the guests departed early, and, as twilight gathered, the happy family sat together round the fire.

"Just a year ago we were groaning over the dismal Christmas we expected to have. Do you remember?" asked Jo.

"Rather a pleasant year on the whole!" said Meg, smiling at the fire.

"I think it's been a pretty hard one," observed Amy, watching the light shine on her ring.

"I'm glad it's over, because we've got you back," whispered Beth, who sat on her father's knee.

"Rather a rough road for you to travel, my little pilgrims. But you have got on bravely; and I think the burdens are in a fair way to tumble off very soon," said Mr. March, looking with fatherly satisfaction at the four young faces gathered round him.

"How do you know? Did mother tell you?" asked Jo.

"Not much; straws show which way the wind blows; and I've made several discoveries today."

"Oh, tell us what they are!" cried Meg.

"Here is one!" and, taking up the hand which lay on the arm of his chair, he pointed to the roughened fore-finger, a burn on the back, and two or three little hard spots on the palm. "I remember a time when this hand was white and smooth, and your first care was to keep it so. It was very pretty then, but to me it's much prettier now."

If Meg had wanted a reward for hours of patient labour, she received it in the hearty pressure of her father's hand.

"What about Jo? Please say something nice; for she has tried so hard, and been so very, very good to me," said Beth in her father's ear.

He laughed, and looked across at the tall girl who sat opposite, with an unusually mild expression on her brown face.

"In spite of the curly crop, I don't see the 'son Jo,' whom I left a year ago," said Mr. March. "I see a young lady who pins her collar straight, laces her boots neatly, and neither whistles, talks slang, nor lies on the rug, as she used to do. Her face is rather thin and pale, just now, with watching and anxiety; but I like to look at it, for it has grown gentler, and her voice is lower; she doesn't bounce, but moves quietly, and takes care of a certain little person in a motherly way. I rather miss my wild girl; but if I get a strong, helpful, tender-hearted woman in her place, I shall feel quite satisfied. I don't know whether shearing sobered our black sheep, but I do know that in all Washington I couldn't find anything beautiful enough to be bought with the five-and-twenty dollars which my good girl sent me."

Jo's keen eyes were rather dim for a minute, and her thin face grew rosy in the firelight, as she received her father's praise.

"Now, Beth," said Amy, longing for her turn.

"There's so little of her I'm afraid to say much, for fear she will slip away altogether, though she is not so shy as she used to be," began their father cheerfully; but, recollecting how nearly he *had* lost her, he held her close, saying tenderly, with her cheek against his own, "I've got you safe, my Beth, and I'll keep you so, please God."

After a minute's silence he looked down at Amy, who sat at his feet, and said, with a caress of the shining hair, — "I observed that Amy took drumsticks at dinner, ran errands for her mother, gave Meg her place to-night, and has waited on everyone with patience and good humour. I also observe that she does not fret much, nor prink at the glass, and has not even mentioned a very pretty ring which she wears; so I conclude that she has learned to think of other people more, and of herself less."

"What are you thinking of, Beth?" asked Jo, when Amy had thanked her father, and told about her ring.

"I read in *Pilgrim's Progress* today how, after many troubles, Christian and Hopeful came to a pleasant green meadow, and there they rested happily, as we do now, before they went on to their journey's end," answered Beth; adding, as she slipped out of her father's arms, and went slowly to the instrument, "It's singing time now, and I want to be in my old place. I'll try to sing the song of the shepherd boy which the Pilgrims heard. I made the music for father, because he likes the verses."

So, sitting at the dear little piano Beth softly touched the keys, and, in the sweet voice they had never thought to hear again, sang, to her own accompaniment, the quaint hymn, which was a singularly fitting song for her: —

> *"He that is down need fear no fall,*
> *He that is low no pride;*
> *He that is humble ever shall*
> *Have God to be his guide.*
>
> *"I am content with what I have,*
> *Little be it or much;*
> *And, Lord! contentment still I crave,*
> *Because Thou savest such.*
>
> *"Fullness to them a burden is,*
> *That go on pilgrimage;*
> *Here little, and hereafter bliss,*
> *Is best from age to age!*

## CHAPTER TWENTY-THREE

## AUNT MARCH SETTLES THE QUESTION

Like bees swarming after their queen, mother and daughters hovered about Mr. March the next day, neglecting everything to look at, wait upon, and listen to the new invalid. As he sat propped up in the big chair by Beth's sofa, with the other three close by, and Hannah popping her head now and then, "to peek at the dear man," nothing seemed needed to complete their happiness. But something *was* needed, and the elder ones felt it, though none confessed the fact. Mr. and Mrs. March looked at one another with an anxious expression, as their eyes followed Meg. Jo had sudden fits of sobriety, and was seen to shake her fist at Mr. Brooke's umbrella, which had been left in the hall; Meg was absent-minded, started when the bell rang, and coloured when John's name was mentioned.

Laurie went by in the afternoon, and, seeing Meg at the window, seemed suddenly possessed with a melodramatic fit, for he fell down upon one knee in the snow, beat his breast, tore his hair, and clasped his hands imploringly; and when Meg told him to behave himself, and go away, he wrung imaginary tears out of his handkerchief, and staggered round the corner as if in utter despair.

"What does the goose mean?" said Meg.

"He's showing you how your John will go on by-and-by. Touching, isn't it?" answered Jo scornfully.

"Don't say *my John;* it isn't proper or true"; but Meg's voice lingered over the words as if they sounded pleasant to her. "Please don't plague me, Jo; I've told you I don't care *much* about him, and there isn't to be anything said, but we are all to be friendly, and go on as before."

"We can't, for something *has* been said, and Laurie's mischief has spoilt you for me. I see it, and so does mother; you are not like your own self a bit, and seem ever so far away from me. I don't mean to plague you, and will bear it like a man, but I do wish it was all settled. I hate to wait; so if you mean ever to do it, make haste and have it over quick," said Jo pettishly.

"I cant's say or do anything till he speaks, and he won't because father said I was too young," began Meg.

"If he did speak you wouldn't know what to say, but would cry or blush, or let him have his own way, instead of giving a good decided No."

"I'm not so silly and weak as you think. I know just what I should say, for I've planned it all; there's no knowing what may happen, and I wished to be prepared."

"Would you mind telling me what you'd say?" asked Jo, more respectfully.

"Oh, I should merely say, quite calmly and decidedly, 'Thank you, Mr. Brooke, you are very kind, but I agree with father that I am too young to enter into any engagement at present; so please say no more, but let us be friends as we were.'"

"I don't believe you'll ever say it, and I know he won't be satisfied if you do. If he goes on like the rejected lovers in books, you'll give in, rather than hurt his feelings."

"No, I won't! I shall tell him I've made up my mind, and shall walk out of the room with dignity."

Meg rose as she spoke, and was just going to rehearse the dignified exit, when a step in the hall made her fly into her seat, and begin to sew as if her life depended on finishing that particular seam in a given time. Jo smothered a laugh at the sudden change, and, when someone gave a modest tap, opened the door with grim aspect.

"Good-afternoon, I came to get my umbrella — that is, to see how your father finds himself today," said Mr. Brooke, getting a trifle confused.

"It's very well, he's in the rack, I'll get him, and tell it you are there"; and having jumbled her father and the umbrella well together in her reply, Jo slipped out of the room to give Meg a chance to make her speech, and air her dignity. But the instant she vanished, Meg began to sidle towards the door, murmuring, — "Mother will like to see you; pray sit down, I'll call her."

"Don't go; are you afraid of me, Margaret?" and Mr. Brooke looked so hurt that Meg thought she must have done something very rude. She blushed up to the little curls on her forehead, for he had never called her Margaret before. Anxious to appear friendly and at her ease, she put out her hand with a confiding gesture, and said gratefully, "How can I be afraid when you have been so kind to father? I only with I could thank you for it."

"Shall I tell you how?" asked Mr. Brooke, holding the small hand fast in both his big ones, and looking down at Meg with so much love in his brown eyes that her heart began to flutter.

"Oh, no, please don't — I'd rather not," she said, trying to withdraw her hand, and looking frightened.

"I won't trouble you; I only want to know if you care for me a little, Meg; I love you so much, dear," added Mr. Brooke tenderly.

This was the moment for the calm, proper speech, but Meg didn't make it, she forgot every word of it, hung her head, and answered, "I don't know," so softly that John had to stoop down to catch the foolish little reply.

He seemed to think it was worth the trouble, for he smiled to himself as if quite satisfied, pressed the plump hand gracefully, and said in his most persuasive tone, "Will you try to find out? I want to know so much; for I can't go to work with any heart until I learn whether I am to have my reward in the end or not."

"I'm too young," faltered Meg.

"I'll wait; and in the meantime you could be learning to like me. Would it be a very hard lesson, dear?"

"Not if I choose to learn it; but —"

"Please choose to learn, Meg. I love to teach, and this is easier than German," broke in John, getting possession of the other hand, so that she had no way of hiding her face.

His tone was properly beseeching; but, stealing a shy look at him, Meg saw that his eyes were merry as well as tender, and that he wore the satisfied smile of one who had no doubt of his success. This nettled her; Annie Moffat's foolish lessons in coquetry came into her mind, and the love of power, which sleeps in the bosoms of the best of little women, woke up all of a sudden, and took possession of her. She felt excited and strange, and, not knowing what else to do, followed a capricious impulse, and, withdrawing her hands, said petulantly, "I *don't* choose; please go away; and let me be!"

Poor Mr. Brooke looked as if his lovely castle in the air was tumbling about his ears, for he had never seen Meg in such a mood before, and it rather bewildered him.

"Do you really mean that?" he asked, anxiously following her as she walked away.

"Yes, I do; I don't want to be worried about such things. Father says I needn't; it's too soon, and I'd rather not."

"Mayn't I hope you'll change your mind by-and-by? I'll wait and say nothing till you have had more time. Don't play with me, Meg. I didn't think that of you."

"Don't think of me at all. I'd rather you wouldn't," said Meg, taking a naughty satisfaction in trying her lover's patience and her own power.

He was grave and pale now, and looked decidedly more like the novel heroes whom she admired; but he neither slapped his forehead nor tramped about the room, as they did; he just stood looking at her so wistfully, so tenderly, that she found her heart relenting in spite of herself. What would have happened next I cannot say, if Aunt March had not come hobbling in.

The old lady couldn't resist her longing to see her nephew; for she had met Laurie as she took her airing, and, hearing of Mr. March's arrival, drove straight out to see him. The family were all busy in the back part of the house, and she had made her way quietly in, hoping to surprise them. She did surprise two of them so much that Meg started as if she had seen a ghost, and Mr. Brooke vanished into the study.

"Bless me! what's all this?" cried the old lady, with a rap of her cane, as she glanced from the pale young gentleman to the scarlet young lady.

"It's father's friend. I'm so surprised to see you," stammered Meg.

"That's evident," returned Aunt March, sitting down. "But what is father's friend saying to make you look like a peony? There's mischief going on, and I insist upon knowing what it is!"

"We were merely talking. Mr. Brooke came for his umbrella," began Meg.

"Brooke? That boy's tutor? Ah! I understand now. Jo blundered into a wrong message in one of your pa's letters, and I made her tell me. You haven't gone and accepted him, child?" cried Aunt March.

"Hush! he'll hear! Shan't I call mother?" said Meg, much troubled.

"Not yet. I've something to say to you, and I must free my mind at once. Tell me, do you mean to marry this Cook? If you do, not one penny of my money ever goes to you. Remember that, and be a sensible girl," said the old lady.

Now Aunt March possessed, in perfection, the art of rousing the spirit of opposition in the gentlest people. If Aunt March had begged Meg to accept John Brooke, she would probably have declared she couldn't think of it; but, as she was ordered *not* to like him, she immediately made up her mind that she would. Inclination as well as perversity made the decision easy, and, being already much excited, Meg opposed the old lady with unusual spirit.

"I shall marry whom I please, Aunt March, and you can leave your money to anyone you like."

"Highty tighty! Is that the way you take my advice, miss? You'll be sorry for it by-and-by when you've tried love in a cottage, and found it a failure."

"It can't be a worse one than some people find in big houses," retorted Meg.

Aunt March put on her glasses and took a look at the girl, for she did not know her in this new mood. Meg hardly knew herself, she felt so brave and independent — so glad to defend John, and assert her right to love him if she liked. Aunt March saw that she had begun wrong, and, after a little pause, made a fresh start, saying, as mildly as she could, "Now, Meg my dear, be reasonable, and take my advice. You ought to marry well, and help your family; it's your duty to make a rich match."

"Father and mother don't think so; they like John, though he *is* poor."

"Your pa and ma, my dear, have no more worldly wisdom than two babies."

"I'm glad of it," cried Meg, stoutly.

Aunt March took no notice, but went on with her lecture.

"This Rook is poor, and hasn't got any rich relations, has he?"

"No, but he has many warm friends."

"You can't live on friends; try it, and see how cool they'll grow. He hasn't any business, has he?"

"Not yet; Mr. Laurence is going to help him."

"That won't last long. James Laurence is a crotchety old fellow, and not to be depended on. So you intend to marry a man without money, position, or business, and go on working harder than you do now, when you might be comfortable all your days by minding me, and going better? I thought you had more sense, Meg."

"I couldn't do better if I waited half my life! John is good and wise; he's got heaps of talent; he's willing to work, and sure to get on, he's so energetic and brave. Everyone likes and respects him, and I'm proud to think he cares for me, though I'm so poor and young, and silly," said Meg, looking prettier than ever in her earnestness.

"He knows *you* have got rich relations, child; that's the secret of his liking I suspect."

"Aunt March, how dare you say such a thing! John is above such meanness, and I won't listen to you a minute if you talk so," cried Meg indignantly, forgetting everything but the injustice of the old lady's suspicions. "My John wouldn't marry for money any more than I would. We are willing to work, and we mean to wait. I'm not afraid of being poor, for I've been happy so far, and I know I shall be with him, because he loves me, and I —"

194

Meg stopped there, remembering, all of a sudden, that she had not made up her mind; that she had told "her John" to go away, and that he might be overhearing her inconsistent remarks.

Aunt March was very angry, for she had set her heart on having her pretty niece make a fine match, and something in the girl's happy young face made the lonely old woman feel sad and sour.

"Well, I wash my hands of the whole affair! You are a wilful child, and you've lost more than you know by this piece of folly. No, I won't stop; I'm disappointed in you, and haven't spirits to see your pa now. Don't expect anything from me when you are married; your Mr. Brooke's friends must take care of you. I'm done with you for ever."

And, slamming the door in Meg's face, Aunt March drove off in high dudgeon. She seemed to take all the girl's courage with her; for, when left alone, Meg stood a moment undecided whether to laugh or cry. Before she could make up her mind, she was taken possession of by Mr. Brooke, who said, all in one breath, "I couldn't help hearing, Meg. Thank you for defending me, and Aunt March for proving that you *do* care for me a little bit."

"I didn't know how much till she abused you," began Meg.

"And I needn't go away, but may stay and be happy — may I, dear?"

Here was another fine chance to make the crushing speech and the stately exit, but Meg never thought of doing either, and disgraced herself in Jo's eyes for ever by meekly whispering, "Yes, John," and hiding her face on Mr. Brooke's waistcoat.

Fifteen minutes after Aunt March's departure, Jo came softly downstairs, paused an instant at the parlour door, and hearing no sound within, nodded and smiled, with a satisfied expression, saying to herself, "She has sent him away as we planned, and that affair is settled. I'll go and hear the fun, and have a good laugh over it."

But poor Jo never got her laugh, for she was transfixed upon the threshold by a spectacle which held her there staring with her mouth nearly as wide open as her eyes. Going in to exult over a fallen enemy, and to praise a strong-minded sister for the banishment of an objectionable lover, it certainly *was* a shock to behold the aforesaid enemy serenely sitting on the sofa, with the strong-minded sister enthroned upon his knee, and wearing an expression of the most abject submission. Jo gave a sort of gasp, as if a cold shower-bath had suddenly fallen upon her — for such an unexpected turning of the tables actually took her breath away. At the odd sound, the lovers turned and saw her. Meg jumped up, looking both proud and shy; but, "that man," as Jo called him, actually laughed, and said coolly, as he kissed the astonished newcomer, "Sister Jo, congratulate us."

That was adding insult to injury! It was altogether too much! and, making some wild demonstration with her hands, Jo vanished without a word. Rushing upstairs, she startled the invalids by exclaiming, tragically, as she burst into the room, "Oh, *do* somebody go down quick! John Brooke is acting dreadfully, and Meg likes it!"

Mr. and Mrs. March left the room with speed; and casting herself upon the bed, Jo cried and scolded tempestuously as she told the awful news to Beth and Amy. The little girls, however, considered it a most agreeable and interesting event, and Jo got little comfort from them; so she went up to her refuge in the garret, and confided her troubles to the rats.

Nobody ever knew what went on in the parlour that afternoon; but a great deal of talking was done, and quiet Mr. Brooke astonished his friends by the eloquence and spirit with which he pleaded his suit, told his plans, and persuaded them to arrange everything just as he wanted it.

The tea-bell rang before he had finished describing the paradise which he meant to earn for Meg, and he proudly took her in to supper, both looking so happy that Jo hadn't the heart to be jealous or dismal.

"You can't say 'nothing pleasant ever happens now,' can you, Meg?" said Amy, trying to decide how she would group the lovers in the sketch she was planning to take.

"No, I'm sure I can't. How much has happened since I said that! It seems a year ago," answered Meg.

"The joys came close up on the sorrows this time, and I rather think the changes have begun," said Mrs. March. "In most families there comes, now and then, a year full of events; this has been such a one, but it ends well, after all."

"Hope the next will end better," muttered Jo, who found it very hard to see Meg absorbed in a stranger before her face; for Jo loved a few persons very dearly, and dreaded to have their affection lost or lessened in any way.

"I hope the third year from this *will* end better; I mean it shall, if I live to work out my plans," said Mr. Brooke, smiling at Meg, as if everything had become possible to him now.

"Doesn't it seem very long to wait?" asked Amy, who was in a hurry for the wedding.

"I've got so much to learn before I shall be ready, it seems a short time to me," answered Meg, with a sweet gravity in her face never seen there before.

"You have only to wait. I am to do the work, said John beginning his labours by picking up Meg's napkin, with an expression which caused Jo to shake her head, and then say to herself with an air of relief, as the front door banged, "Here comes Laurie; now we shall have a little sensible conversation."

But Jo was mistaken; for Laurie came prancing in overflowing with spirits, bearing a great bridal-looking bouquet for "Mrs. John Brooke," and evidently labouring under the delusion that the whole affair had been brought about by his excellent management.

"I knew Brooke would have it all his own way, he always does; for when he makes up his mind to accomplish anything, it's done, though the sky falls," said Laurie, when he had presented his offering and his congratulations.

"Much obliged for that recommendation. I take it as a good omen for the future, and invite you to my wedding on the spot," answered Mr. Brooke, who felt at peace with all mankind, even his mischievous pupil.

"I'll come if I'm at the ends of the earth; for the sight of Jo's face alone, on that occasion, would be worth a long journey. You don't look festive ma'am; what's the matter?" asked Laurie, following her into a corner of the parlour, whither all had adjourned to greet Mr. Laurence.

"I don't approve of the match, but I've made up my mind to bear with it, and shall not say a word against it," said Jo solemnly. "You can't know how hard it is for me to give up Meg," she continued, with a little quiver in her voice.

"You don't give her up. You only go halves," said Laurie consolingly.

"It can never be the same again. I've lost my dearest friend," sighed Jo.

"You've got me, anyhow. I'm not good for much, I know; but I'll stand by you, Jo, all the days of my life, upon my word I will!" and Laurie meant what he said.

"I know you will, and I'm ever so much obliged; you are always a great comfort to me, Teddy," returned Jo, gratefully shaking hands.

"Well, now, don't be dismal, there's a good fellow. It's all right, you see. Meg is happy; Brooke will fly round and get settled immediately; grandpa will attend to him, and it will be very jolly to see Meg in her own little house. We'll have capital times after she is gone, for I shall be through college before long, and then we'll go abroad, or some nice trip or other. Wouldn't that console you?"

"I rather think it would; but there's no knowing what may happen in three years," said Jo thoughtfully.

"That's true! don't you wish you could take a look forward, and see where we shall all be then? I do," returned Laurie.

"I think not, for I might see something sad; and everyone looks so happy now, I don't believe they could be much improved," and Jo's eyes went slowly round the room, brightening as they looked, for the prospect was a pleasant one.

Father and mother sat together, quietly re-living the first chapter of the romance which for them began some twenty years ago. Amy was drawing the lovers, who sat apart in a beautiful world of their own, the light of which touched their face with a grace the little artist could not copy. Beth lay on her sofa talking cheerily with her old friend, who held her little hand as if he felt that it possessed the power to lead him along the peaceful ways she walked. Jo lounged in her favourite low seat with the grave, quiet look which best became her; and Laurie, leaning on the back of her chair, his chin on a level with her curly head, smiled with his friendliest aspect, and nodded at her in the long glass which reflected them both.

So grouped, the curtain falls upon Meg, Jo, Beth and Amy. Whether it ever rises again depends upon the reception given to the first act of the domestic drama called Little Women.

Abbey